A Glimpse of Disaster

"No problem, Joe," Phil said. "We'll take my car."

But Colin interrupted with, "No, Joe! Don't do it!"

"What did you say?" Joe asked.

Colin swallowed hard. "Nothing. Forget it."

Joe turned to Phil. "Well, come on, then. We have just enough time to get to the chemical place and back before chemistry class starts."

When Frank turned back to Colin, Colin had disappeared.

Frank hurried to the end of the hall, but Colin was nowhere in sight. Frank tried the restroom. He found Colin inside, washing his face with cold water.

"Colin! You have to tell me!" Frank said. "What did you mean when you told Joe not to go with Phil?"

"I saw a bad car wreck," Colin managed to say. "I don't think Joe and Phil will make it back alive."

The Hardy Boys Mystery Stories

Available from ALADDIN Paperbacks

THE **HARDY BOYS**®

#177
THE CASE OF THE PSYCHIC'S VISION

FRANKLIN W. DIXON

Aladdin Paperbacks

New York London Toronto Sydney Singapore

First Aladdin Paperbacks edition February 2003

Copyright © 2003 by Simon & Schuster, Inc.

ALADDIN PAPERBACKS
An imprint of Simon & Schuster
Children's Publishing Division
1230 Avenue of the Americas
New York, NY 10020

The text of this book was set in New Caledonia.

Printed in the United States of America
2   4   6   8   10   9   7   5   3   1

THE HARDY BOYS MYSTERY STORIES is a trademark of
Simon & Schuster, Inc.

THE HARDY BOYS and colophon
are registered trademarks of Simon & Schuster, Inc.

Library of Congress Control Number 2002107369

ISBN 0-689-85597-4

Contents

THE CASE OF THE
PSYCHIC'S VISION

1 We're Going to a Séance

"Frank! Joe!" Callie Shaw's voice barely carried over the din of students rushing to change classes at Bayport High School. "Wait up!"

Frank Hardy and his brother, Joe, turned to see Callie hurriedly making her way toward them through the crowded hallway.

"You'll never believe it!" Callie said excitedly. "You'll just never believe it!"

They had to flatten themselves against the wall so they wouldn't get crushed.

"Believe what?" Frank said. He looked at his watch. "Whatever it is, Callie, you need to get it out, because I can't be late to English today."

"I'm having a few friends over at my house

tonight," Callie whispered, "and we're going to have a séance."

"A *séance*?" Joe exclaimed. "Isn't that where you try to contact dead people?"

"Yeah, Callie," Frank said. "What's gotten into you? Why do you want to have a séance?"

"I think it'll be fun," Callie explained. The hallway had cleared some, so they started toward their classrooms. "I thought you'd be excited."

"I don't have time to talk to the live people I know," Joe joked. He grinned at Callie. "I wouldn't know what to say to a dead person."

"Don't be too hard on her, Joe," Frank said. "If Callie wants to have a séance, then let her."

They had arrived at Joe's chemistry classroom.

"But don't tell anyone, okay, Joe?" Callie said, turning to go down the hall to her math class. "Nella Randles doesn't want anyone to know."

Frank shook his head and rolled his eyes. "See you later," he said to Joe.

"Wait up, Frank!" Joe called to him. "Isn't Colin Randles in your English class?"

"Yeah," Frank replied. "Why?"

"See if there's some way you can find out about this séance over at Callie's house," Joe said. "I want to know why Callie doesn't want to talk about it, if it's just going to be something they do for fun."

"That should be easy," Frank said. "Colin's my partner for our new project."

Ms. Long, their English teacher, had assigned each person in her class to be a famous character in history. Partners would interview each other and write up the interview. Frank was Charlemagne and Colin was Geronimo. Ms. Long was only going to give them the first part of the hour for the interview. They had to ask all the pertinent questions during that time. During the second half of the class, they had to write up their interview and turn it in.

"Any questions, class?" Ms. Long asked.

No one had any questions. Everyone was ready to start, because there wasn't much time.

Frank walked over to the empty desk next to Colin.

"Do you want me to interview you first?" Colin asked. His pen was poised over his notebook.

"No, I'll start," Frank said.

He looked around the room to see if anybody was paying attention to them. No one was. They were too engrossed with their interviews. Ms. Long was busy grading papers. For just a second, Frank wondered if he really should say anything to Colin about the séance, but then he remembered that technically it was Joe Callie had asked not to tell. She hadn't said anything to Frank.

"Why is your sister holding a séance at Callie's house tonight?" he whispered.

Colin blanched. For a minute, Frank thought he was going to have some kind of an attack. "You don't know what you're talking about," Colin finally managed to say. "Nella wouldn't do that. Mom and Dad . . ."

Colin stopped. He looked at his watch. "We'll never make it, Hardy, if you don't start asking me Geronimo questions."

"We'll make it, Colin," Frank assured him. "I just want to know about the séance."

"Listen, Frank, it's not something I'm supposed to talk about," Colin finally whispered, "but you're my friend, so I'll talk to you about it after class. I just don't want to do it now, okay?"

Frank took a deep breath. "Okay. I'm sorry I pushed you."

They rushed through the Geronimo and Charlemagne questions, then spent the remainder of the time writing up their interviews. True to Frank's word, they even finished before the hour was up.

When the bell rang, they walked up to Ms. Long's desk together and handed in their interviews.

"I brought my lunch. I usually find someplace quiet to eat," Colin said. "I'll share with you, if you don't mind tuna fish, and I'll tell you why I was so upset in class."

"I can stand tuna fish long enough to hear what you have to say," Frank said. He usually sat with Joe and some of their friends during lunch, but he wanted to learn more about the séance.

Outside, Frank followed Colin to a secluded

part of the high school campus. They sat down on a seldom-used loading dock.

"We have a lot of fun in the cafeteria," Frank said. "You should join us sometimes."

"I like to be by myself," Colin said. "To think."

Frank didn't want this conversation to get too philosophical, so he moved it along. "What about the séance, Colin? Does your sister do this often? I don't think I've ever known anybody who could contact dead people."

For a minute, Colin didn't say anything, but then he gave Frank a wan smile. "Do you think you really know everything about all of your friends, Frank? Do you think they always tell you their secrets?"

Frank shrugged. "Well, yeah, I think so. I guess so. We usually tell each other what's on our minds." He shrugged again. He had suddenly remembered that he didn't always tell his parents or Joe or his friends *everything* that was on his mind. "But this is different, Colin. This is something pretty big."

Colin took a deep breath. "Do you know why my family moved here?"

Frank shook his head.

"So we could have a normal life, that's why. My family is psychic," Colin said. "Mom and Dad used to go around the country, giving psychic readings for people."

"What do you mean?" Frank asked.

"They'd tell people how to invest their money. They'd tell people whether they should marry or not," Colin said. "Stuff like that."

"You mean they're fortune-tellers?" Frank said.

Colin shook his head. "People usually think of frauds when they hear that term," he said. "No, my parents are for real, but eventually, they always seemed to have problems wherever we lived. Some people get really upset about this type of thing, so we'd have to move."

"Are they giving psychic readings here in Bayport?" Frank asked.

Colin shook his head. "No, they're just trying to find regular jobs, because we want to have a regular life." He sighed. "My parents are going to be really upset if they find out that Nella is going to hold a séance."

"I guess I really wasn't supposed to tell," Frank said. "It's just that . . . , well, for some reason I can't explain, I just had to know more about it."

Colin opened his mouth, shut it for a second, then opened it again. "Have you ever thought you were . . . *psychic*, Frank?"

Frank blinked. "No, not me! That's crazy. I was just . . ."

Colin looked at him but didn't say anything.

"Don't tell your parents about Nella," Frank said. "I don't want to get her into trouble."

Colin shrugged. "I guess she agreed to do it

because she wants to make friends. We've moved around so much these last few years that we never had time to make friends." He sighed. "I guess it'll be all right, but I'm going to talk to her myself. She shouldn't be doing this."

The bell to end first lunch rang, and Colin and Frank headed back into the building.

Colin had trigonometry, and Frank had physical education, so they started to separate at the first hall.

But Colin stopped. "What if I told you that there was somebody in this school who was kidnapped when he or she was young and doesn't realize that it happened?" With that, Colin turned and walked away.

Frank could only stare at him as he disappeared around a corner.

Chet Morton, one of the boys' best friends, and Joe met Frank at the door to the locker room.

"Guess what we're going to do tonight?" Chet whispered to Frank.

"What?" Frank asked.

"We're going to a séance," Joe said.

Frank stopped and looked at Joe. "Callie told you not to tell anyone about this," he said, remembering that he was guilty of the same thing by talking to Colin.

"I didn't tell Chet," Joe explained. "Iola did."

"Iola is going to Callie's house. That new girl,

Nella what's-her-name, uh, Randles is going to hold a séance," Chet said. "We're going to make *sure* they contact some dead people."

Chet Morton was always playing practical jokes on people, but Frank wasn't sure he wanted to go along with this one.

Frank opened the locker-room door. "I thought we were going to that new movie at the multiplex," he said.

"Nah," Chet said. "This will be more fun."

Joe agreed.

They had made it to the dressing room and were putting on their running shorts.

"Okay," Frank said. "Count me in."

He was afraid that if he didn't agree, Chet would keep talking about it, and Frank didn't want the rest of the guys in the locker room to know about the séance. *If I'm at Callie's,* Frank thought, *I can make sure that things don't get out of hand.*

When Frank finally finished changing, he joined the rest of the group as it headed out to the track. Just outside the door of the dressing room, he felt something brush against the back of his neck. It sent chills up his spine.

Frank turned around to see who had touched him. But there was nobody there.

2 Psychic Detectives

"Do you really think we can make it to State Championships, Frank?" Joe asked as Frank drove the van toward their house.

They were later than usual, because Coach Bradley, the new track and field coach, had asked them if they could stay for a few minutes after practice. He had some pointers to give Frank on how to throw the javelin, and he wanted to discuss standing broad-jump techniques with Joe.

"Coach sure seems to think so," Frank said as he turned onto High Street and headed the two blocks to Elm.

"Well, he may be right," Joe mused. "Chet's got the shot put down. Tony Prito can beat anybody in the one-hundred meters. Phil Cohen never misses a hurdle. And Biff Hooper keeps breaking his own pole vault records."

"Good!" Frank said, as they turned into their driveway. "Dad's home."

"Weren't you listening to me, Frank?" Joe complained. "This is very important, you know."

"Yes, Joe, I was listening, and I know winning States in track and field is important," Frank said as he parked the van behind their mother's car, "but I can't get that séance out of my mind. I have some things I want to ask Dad about it." Fenton Hardy was a well-known and very successful private investigator in Bayport.

"Hey! The séance! I almost forgot!" Joe said as he jumped out of the van. "We're going to play that joke on the girls tonight."

Frank didn't say anything. But something about Chet's plan was making him uneasy.

Inside the house, the boys quickly headed to the dining room. Mr. and Mrs. Hardy and Aunt Gertrude had already started eating.

"Sorry we're late," Frank said.

"Our new track and field coach thinks we're headed to States," Joe added. "He was just fine-tuning our techniques, and we lost track of the time."

"No problem. We thought it was probably something like that," Mrs. Hardy said. "Wash up and sit down before dinner gets cold."

"You two have cell phones, don't you?" Aunt Gertrude said. "Since you're paying good money for the service, you might think about using them to let people know if you're going to be late."

Joe looked at Frank, grinned, and rolled his eyes. They both loved their Aunt Gertrude, but she never minced words. You always knew exactly how she felt about everything.

"They were in our lockers inside the dressing room, Aunt Gertrude," Frank explained. "We were outside on the track."

"Yeah! The coach doesn't like us talking on cell phones during the middle of a practice, Aunt Gertrude," Joe explained, then shrugged. "What could we do?"

Aunt Gertrude narrowed her eyes at him.

Fenton Hardy gave both the boys a look that said, "Let's drop this subject and eat."

Since the boys had already showered and changed clothes at school, all they had to do was wash their hands, which they did at the kitchen sink, and sit down at the table.

"I'm starved," Joe said. "Standing broad jumps really make you work up an appetite."

Frank helped himself to some mashed potatoes and said, "Dad, what do you think about psychic detection?"

Aunt Gertrude had been taking a drink of water and almost choked.

"Gertrude! Are you all right?" Mrs. Hardy had come over to where Aunt Gertrude was sitting and was patting her sister-in-law on the back.

Finally, Aunt Gertrude managed to say, "Laura! You're beating me to death! Stop that! Please! I'm okay!"

"Sorry, Gertrude, but you scared me," Mrs. Hardy said, and sat back down. "You were starting to turn purple."

"Well, I'm okay now," Aunt Gertrude said. She took a slow sip of water and looked at Frank but didn't say anything.

"Psychic detection," Fenton Hardy repeated. "It's interesting that you mention that just now, Frank."

"Why, Dad?" Joe asked.

"Well, a lot of police departments around the country, including the one right here in Bayport, will call in psychic detectives from time to time," Mr. Hardy explained, "but they don't like to talk about it."

"Why not?" Frank asked.

"There are lots of reasons," Mr. Hardy said. "I think the main one is pride. Police departments like to think they can solve crimes on their own, using accepted police procedures."

"What can psychic detectives do that the police can't?" Joe asked.

"From what I understand, and I'm really no

authority on it," Fenton Hardy began, "psychics will experience clairvoyance, clairaudience, clairsentience, and clairolfactance all at the same time."

Mrs. Hardy stood up. "This conversation is getting too spooky for me. Shall we, Gertrude?" she added.

"Not just yet, Laura," Aunt Gertrude said. "I want to hear the rest of this."

Frank looked at his aunt. *That's interesting*, he thought. *Usually, Aunt Gertrude dismisses things like this.*

"Clairvoyance is when a psychic sees things. Clairaudience is when a psychic hears things," Mr. Hardy continued. "Clairsentience is when a psychic can gather certain information just by touching an object. This is more commonly known as psychometry. And clairolfactance is when the psychic gets information through smell."

"Do you really believe all of this, Fenton?" Aunt Gertrude suddenly asked her brother.

"Do I believe this, Gertrude?" Mr. Hardy said. "Well, if I can't disprove it on my own, then I don't say I disbelieve it. I may be skeptical, but I always try to keep an open mind. That's what's important. I just don't know. I don't think anybody really knows."

"Have you ever used a psychic to help you solve a crime, Dad?" Joe asked.

Frank thought he saw a slight blush come to his father's face, but he couldn't be sure.

Mr. Hardy smiled. "Well, as a matter of fact I did once," he said.

There was an audible gasp from Mrs. Hardy, who had come back into the dining room.

"Fenton, I didn't know that," she said. "You never told me. When did it happen?"

Mr. Hardy turned to the boys and Aunt Gertrude. "Your mother's reaction is typical. For some reason, psychics scare people. I think it's because we all have a fear of the unknown." He turned to his wife. "It was a couple of years ago, Laura. I was really stumped by the Marston case."

"I remember that," Frank said. "Missing diamonds."

"Right," Mr. Hardy said. "I was talking to Chief Collig about it and he just happened to mention a psychic who had helped him solve a similar case two years before."

"Chief Collig uses psychics?" Joe exclaimed.

"That information is not to leave this room, Joe," Mr. Hardy said. "Chief Collig told me that in confidence and I expect my family to keep the confidence. I only mentioned it to you because you boys have been involved in solving a lot of crimes and you understand these things."

"Right," Frank and Joe said in unison.

"The psychic was a man named Wilson Chatham. He lives about thirty miles from Bayport, in Brandstone," Mr. Hardy explained. "I contacted him and he agreed to use psychometry. That's when a psychic takes something that belonged to the victim, in this case, a leather drawstring bag that held the diamonds, and touches it to get information. Research has shown that in times of great stress, such as when somebody is stealing a fortune from you, your energy merges with the energy of the object, the bag, and leaves a memory trace. I don't know enough about this to explain it very well, but the psychic can pick up on that memory and give the police—or in my case, a private investigator—all kinds of clues."

"It worked?" Joe asked.

Mr. Hardy nodded. "I got enough information from Chatham to locate the diamonds and return them to their owner."

Just then, the telephone rang.

"I'll get it," Joe said. He excused himself from the table and grabbed the extension in the kitchen.

"Hey, Joe! It's Chet! Are you guys ready?"

"Ready?" Joe said.

"We're going over to Callie's, remember?" Chet said. "We're going to make sure this is a séance they'll *never* forget."

Joe couldn't believe that he had forgotten about the séance again, but just listening to his father talk about using psychics to solve mysteries had taken his mind off it.

"Yeah, sure! Frank's finishing up dinner," Joe

said. "Are you coming by or do you want us to pick you up?"

"I'll be by," Chet said. "It's just going to be the three of us."

"What happened to the rest of the gang?" Joe asked.

"They chickened out," Chet said. "I think they got spooked."

I can almost understand that, Joe thought. "Well, we're still on," he said to Chet.

"I'll be by in about ten minutes," Chet said. "I'll honk."

"Okay," Joe said and hung up the receiver.

He had just started back into the dining room, when the telephone rang again.

"What is it?" Joe said into the receiver. He was sure it was Chet again. "Do you want me to bring you what we didn't eat for dinner?"

But Joe heard only a crackling noise on the other end before a voice said in a low whisper, "Don't go to that séance. If you do, you won't leave there alive."

Then there was a click and the line went dead.

3 Attacked!

Just then Frank came into the kitchen, carrying some dirty plates and bowls. "Who was that on the phone?"

"The first call was from Chet," Joe said. "He'll be by to pick us up in a few minutes."

"I don't know, Joe. Do you really think this is a good idea?" Frank asked. "Maybe we should be more serious about what psychics do. Dad certainly is."

"Ask me about the second call," Joe said.

Frank gave him a puzzled look. "Okay," he said. "Who was the second call from?"

Joe shrugged. "I didn't recognize the voice, but whoever it was said if we went to the séance, we wouldn't leave alive." He grinned at Frank. "So I'm definitely going. No threat is going to scare me away from this now."

Frank put the dishes by the sink. "Good call," he said.

Just then, Aunt Gertrude and Mrs. Hardy came into the kitchen, so the boys cut short their conversation.

"We're going over to Callie Shaw's for a little while, Mom," Frank said. "We'll be back later."

"Okay, boys," Mrs. Hardy said.

Frank and Joe headed through the house.

"Do you think we should tell Dad about the séance, nothing about the practical joke, but maybe just to let him know what's going on?" Joe said.

"Maybe we should," Frank agreed. "I'd like to hear what he has to say."

But Mr. Hardy had already gone into his study, closing the door, which was a signal to the rest of the family that he was hard at work on a case and didn't want to be disturbed unless it was an emergency. Frank and Joe both agreed that this probably wasn't an emergency.

They had just stepped outside when Chet pulled into the driveway. The boys ran out to Chet's car and got inside.

As Chet backed out of the driveway he said, "Are you guys ready for some fun? I've been thinking of all the things we can do over at Callie's house. We're going to freak those girls out!"

When neither Frank nor Joe said anything, Chet asked, "What's the matter?"

"Joe received a threatening phone call before we left," Frank told him. "Whoever it was said we'd never leave Callie's house alive."

"Yeah, right," Chet said. He looked over at Joe. "Who do you think called?"

"I didn't recognize the voice," Joe said. "The person was whispering."

"I wonder if it was Colin Randles," Frank said.

"Nella's brother?" Chet said.

"Yeah. We talked today," Frank said. "I just haven't had time to . . ."

All of a sudden, headlights from behind blinded them.

"What's wrong with that stupid driver?" Chet said. "He's got his brights on, and he's tailgating me."

"Speed up," Frank said. "You're only going thirty and you can go forty-five on this street."

Chet sped up. "I'll put an end to this," he said.

He turned a corner rapidly, but so did the car that was following them.

Inside Chet's car, it was almost as bright as day.

"We can take the expressway to Callie's house," Joe said. "You should be able to lose them there."

"It's hard to see," Chet said. "Maybe I should pull over and let them pass."

"No! It could be a carjacking," Joe said. "Dad said there was one in downtown Bayport just last week."

19

"Joe's right, Chet," Frank said. "You've got those fancy rims on your wheels; they might want those. I wouldn't pull over. I'd try to lose them."

Up ahead, they saw the entrance to the expressway.

"Hold on, then!" Chet said.

He floored the gas pedal and shot ahead of the other car. But soon their follower was back on their tail again as they barreled down the expressway.

"There's no way these guys are going to get my rims," Chet announced. "I used up almost all of my savings to buy them."

Still, the car stayed behind them.

"Where's a patrolman when you need one?" Joe said.

"Callie's exit is the next one," Frank said. "Don't signal. Just turn at the last minute."

"Okay! Okay! We're almost there!" Chet said. "Hold on!"

He swerved his car onto the off-ramp and raced down to the service road.

"All right!" Joe shouted. "I think we lost them."

Above them, on the expressway, they could see the car. It was a couple miles away, so they thought they would be long gone before the car made it back to where they were.

"Creeps. Low lifes!" Chet muttered. "Why can't they save their money and buy their own rims?"

"I've been thinking, Chet. Whoever that was may

not have wanted your rims after all," Frank said. "It could be the same person who called Joe and told us not to go to the séance."

"Colin?" Joe asked.

Frank nodded. "The telephone call didn't work, so maybe he thought something like this might."

"I don't get it," Joe said. "If it was Colin, then why is he so uptight about this séance?"

"Wait'll you hear the rest of what I learned about him and his family today," Frank said. He told his friends about his lunchtime conversation with Colin.

When Frank finished, Chet said, "He could have killed us!"

"No. I think he just wanted to scare us away. He's afraid that if all this psychic stuff upsets people, they'll have to leave town again, and he doesn't want to do that," Frank said. "He probably thought that if he could keep us occupied with a chase long enough, we might miss the séance."

"Well, that's not going to happen," Chet said. "There's Callie's house just down the street."

Chet parked in front of the house next door to the Shaw's.

"How are we going to do this?" Joe asked. "We weren't invited to the party. Are we just going to crash it?"

"I've got this all figured out," Chet said.

Frank was sure he did. Chet knew every trick in the book.

Frank and Joe followed Chet around to the side gate of the Shaws' house.

"Iola said they were going to have the séance inside the gazebo in the backyard," Chet said. "Nella told them it has just the right atmosphere."

Good, Frank thought. *Callie's parents might not appreciate having Chet's practical joke carried out in their house.*

Chet slowly opened the side gate. It was dark enough now that they couldn't be seen in the shadows beside the house. The Shaws' backyard was planted with tall leafy trees and thick flowering bushes, which hid them as they headed toward the gazebo at the back of the yard.

All of the spotlights in the backyard were off, too, and the only light was coming from a candle in the center of the gazebo.

Frank could feel the adrenaline flowing. He loved a good practical joke too. He only hoped Callie appreciated it.

Finally they reached the side of the gazebo without being detected.

Through the latticework, Frank saw Callie, Iola, and Nella seated around a table.

"Are you all believers?" Nella was saying.

"Yes," Callie and Iola said.

Suddenly, Iola giggled.

"Iola!" Callie whispered. "Stop!"

"Sorry," Iola said.

"If you do not believe, you will ruin this for everyone," Nella said.

"I believe," Iola managed to say.

"Then listen carefully and concentrate on what we're doing," Nella continued. "We must make sure the spirits have the right atmosphere, or we won't be able to contact them. Do you understand?"

Callie and Iola nodded.

Frank peeked through the latticework again. The flickering candles made strange shapes inside the gazebo and distorted the faces of the girls. Callie had said this was all for fun, as part of the sleepover, but Nella seemed pretty serious about it. No wonder Colin had panicked. Things like this tended to upset certain people in the community—and sometimes those people could cause problems.

Joe heard someone murmuring and thought it had to be Nella. *This must be part of the ceremony,* he thought. He was beginning to feel kind of creepy being there. He looked around, wondering if Nella would be able to attract spirits to the séance, then stopped, surprised at himself for even thinking that.

Suddenly, Nella stopped murmuring. "There are spirits here," she said. "I can feel them."

"Who?" Callie asked.

"Call out some names and see who answers," Nella said.

"Roberta Sanders," Iola said.

The three boys looked at each other. Roberta Sanders was a physical education teacher at Bayport High School. She had gone to South America one summer and just disappeared. A lot of the girls were really upset about it.

Suddenly, Chet said, "I'm here! What do you want?" He used a high-pitched and faraway-sounding voice.

"Oh, my gosh!" Callie cried. "It works!"

That seemed to spur Chet on.

"I heard you calling me from faraway South America," Chet said in his 'spirit' voice. "I've come back to Bayport to answer your questions."

Joe had started to wonder if Chet was going too far. Just as he looked over at Frank to see if he felt the same way, Frank fell to the ground and disappeared around the other side of the gazebo. It was as though someone was dragging him out of sight.

"Frank!" Joe shouted.

On the gazebo, the candle had gone out, and the girls began to scream.

Frank was fighting just to breathe. Someone had grabbed him from behind and had his hands around Frank's throat, choking the life out of him. It was so dark that he couldn't see the person's face, but Frank was sure that he knew who it was.

Finally, Frank managed to flip over onto his back. The person's hands were still around his neck.

Choking. Frank knew he was close to passing out. He couldn't let that happen. With one final push, he managed to shove his attacker off of him.

Frank sat up, gasping for breath. Floodlights lit up the backyard. Mr. and Mrs. Shaw had come outside to see what was going on.

"Is everything all right?" Mr. Shaw shouted.

The girls were all standing together in the center of the gazebo, looking down into the yard, where the three boys were crouched.

"Frank! Joe!" Callie shouted.

"Chet!" Iola shouted. "I should have known!"

Joe was hoping that at least one of the girls would start laughing, but nobody seemed to think there was anything funny about what had happened.

Chet and Joe helped Frank up.

"We just wanted to see what the séance was like," Joe explained lamely. He didn't think this was the time to mention practical jokes. "We didn't mean to scare you."

"Well, you shouldn't have slipped up on us like that," Callie said. "You should have just joined us around the table."

"And you definitely shouldn't have pretended you were Ms. Sanders, Chet," Iola told her brother. "That's just, well, that's just plain sick."

"Sorry," Chet said.

"Nella!"

Everyone turned to see who had come through

the side gate. After a few seconds, Colin Randles walked into the light.

"I need to talk to you!" Frank shouted at him. "You have some explaining to do."

"What do you mean?" Colin said.

"If you'll come closer, I'll show you the bruises your fingers made on my neck," Frank said.

"You're crazy, Hardy!" Colin said.

"Really?" Frank said. "So you deny attacking me just a few minutes ago?"

"Yes, I do," Colin said. "I just got here."

"I don't believe you," Frank said.

Just then, two more people came into the light to stand behind Colin.

"Colin's telling the truth. I'm his father," the man said. "We've come to take Nella home."

Frank was stunned. If Colin hadn't attacked him, then who had?

4 I See Things

"Why don't we all go inside and discuss this?" Mr. Shaw said.

Frank could tell by the expression on Nella's face that she was hoping her parents would accept the invitation. Since the tone of Mr. Shaw's voice was nonthreatening, Mr. and Mrs. Randles agreed.

Once inside, the Shaws made everyone feel at ease. Their large family room was comfortable and already stocked with snacks and cold drinks for Callie's friends.

"Now then," Mr. Shaw began, after everyone had plates piled high with food, "who wants to start?" He was looking at Frank, Joe, and Chet.

"We thought it would be funny to scare the girls

during the séance," Chet volunteered. He shrugged. "I guess it kind of got out of hand."

"Yeah, just a tad," Callie agreed.

Iola was giving her brother a dirty look.

"Who were you fighting with, Frank?" Mrs. Shaw asked.

Frank looked around the room, his eyes finally landing on Colin. He shrugged. "I thought it was Colin, but I guess it wasn't."

"You don't know?" Callie said.

Frank shook his head. "It was dark. When the lights came on, the person was gone."

"It was someone who was visiting the séance," Nella said.

"Nella!" Mrs. Randles said sternly. "Keep quiet."

Mr. and Mrs. Shaw looked at each other.

"It's okay, Mrs. Randles," Mrs. Shaw said. "We're an open-minded family here. We always try to listen, even if we, well, don't always believe everything we hear."

"We moved here to Bayport to get away from all of this," Mr. Randles said. "It's become a curse!"

"What has?" Callie asked.

"Our psychic powers," Mrs. Randles said.

For a few seconds, nobody said anything, then Joe said, "Colin, are you sure you weren't fighting Frank? Somebody was."

Colin took a deep breath. "I called your house and told you not to come to this séance," he admitted, "and I followed you in my car, trying to keep you from coming here. I'm sorry. I know I shouldn't have done either one of those things, but I was not fighting Frank by the gazebo."

"I've already told you that," Mr. Randles said. "Colin came home and told us what he had done and why Nella was here."

"That's why we came over here," Mrs. Randles added. "It was the first we knew about the séance Nella was holding." She looked at her daughter. "Why?"

Nella bowed her head. "I thought it might be a way to make friends fast," she said. "I'm tired of never having any friends."

Callie and Iola went over and put their arms around her. "We'd be friends with you, Nella, even if you didn't hold a séance."

"Some people won't have anything to do with you if you're psychic," Mr. Randles said. "You scare them. So we all agreed to stop. We just wanted the kids to have a normal life."

Frank shook his head. There had to be more to this than he was hearing. Somebody had been fighting him by the gazebo. If it wasn't Colin—and he was almost sure now that it wasn't—then it had to be somebody who had come to Nella's séance. But that would mean he was fighting a person who wasn't . . . *alive*.

Mr. Randles stood up. "We've taken up too much

of your time already," he said. "We need to be going home. I have a job interview in the morning." He turned to Nella. "Get your things," he added.

"Why don't you let her stay?" Mrs. Shaw said. "The girls have been looking forward to this."

"Please, Dad," Nella said.

"I don't think there will be any more séances," Mr. Shaw said. Looking at Frank, Joe, and Chet, he added, "Or young men playing practical jokes around here. Right, Chet?"

"Right," Chet said.

Mr. Shaw turned to Mr. Randles. "What's the job interview you have?"

Mr. Randles named a factory in Bayport. "It's just assembly line work, but it's work, and they may even have something for my wife."

Mr. Shaw thought for a minute. "I've just bought a hardware store here in Bayport, and I'll need a manager and a clerk. Do you two know anything about hardware?"

"Well, we've had to use it a lot, because we've never been able to afford a lot of plumbers or carpenters over the years," Mr. Randles said. He looked at his wife and smiled. "And we're both fast learners."

Mr. Shaw wrote down an address. "I'll meet you here in the morning at nine o'clock. I think this may work out for both of us."

Mr. Randles turned to Nella. "It's all right if you

stay, as long as you girls get some sleep." Nella nodded.

As they headed out of the Shaws' house, Colin came up to Frank. "No hard feelings, Charlemagne?"

Frank grinned. "No hard feelings, Geronimo."

Frank, Joe, and Chet got back into Chet's car, but Frank told Chet to wait until the Randles had already gone.

"Why?" Chet said. "There's no way I'm going to play another prank on anybody!" He grinned. "Not tonight, at least."

"That's what I thought," Joe said. "I didn't think your practical joke playing days were over."

"Not by a long shot, buddy," Chet assured him.

"So, what are we waiting for?" Joe asked Frank.

"There's just something here that's not adding up," Frank said. "I can't believe that Mr. and Mrs. Randles would be so upset about Nella's having a séance at a sleepover. It has to be something bigger."

"Well, they did say that they used to tell fortunes in other towns," Joe reminded him.

"What's the big deal there?" Frank said. "That shouldn't really get people all that riled up. There are a lot of fortune-tellers around. No, it has to be something else. They weren't telling everything they knew about their psychic abilities."

No one said anything.

Finally, Frank said, "I think it has to do with

Colin. He's the only one in the family nobody said anything about."

"What do you mean?" Joe asked.

"I think Colin is the real psychic," Frank explained. "Oh, I don't mean the rest of them aren't. During that séance, *something* attacked me. It could have been sticks and stones blown up by a strong wind, I guess, but what if Nella contacted a really angry spirit? Anyway, I'll wager that séances and fortune-telling are minor compared to Colin's psychic abilities."

"I say we find out," Joe said.

"I say we do, too," Frank agreed.

On Monday morning Frank cornered Colin after English class. "We need to talk."

Colin tried to pull away to his right, but Frank blocked his path.

"I don't have to talk to you, Hardy," Colin said.

When he tried to go to the left, Frank blocked that way, too.

"I didn't take you for a bully, Hardy," Colin said. He was staring directly into Frank's eyes, and there was something very disquieting about it.

"I'm not a bully, Colin," Frank said. He tried to make his tone friendlier. "I'm just trying to find out what's going on here."

"You're asking the wrong person," Colin said. "You need to ask my sister."

Frank looked around. He didn't want Ms. Long or anyone else to hear him. "I don't think I am, Colin. Nella may be able to call up spirits at séances and your parents may be able to tell fortunes, but I think it's your psychic ability that your family is really worried about. What are you not telling people?"

Colin took a deep breath and once again stared darkly into Frank's eyes.

"I see things that other people don't see, Frank," Colin whispered. "I see other's people's secrets."

Frank stepped back, stunned.

"Satisfied?" Colin said.

Just as he started to leave, Joe came up with Phil Cohen.

"Our chemistry teacher needs some chemicals for an experiment we're doing in the lab this afternoon," Joe said. "Phil and I are driving over to a chemical supply company to pick them up. We both have study hall now, and the principal said we could. I'm taking the van."

"You can't do that," Frank said. "I promised the coach I'd pick up a couple of new hurdles at that big sports warehouse just outside of town. I'll need the van for that."

"No problem, Joe," Phil said. "We'll take my car."

Joe wasn't sure that was such a great idea, because Phil sometimes drove too fast. Since he had gotten his new sports car, he was about to set a record at Bayport High School for receiving the most speeding tickets.

"Well, I guess—," Joe started to say.

But Colin interrupted with, "No, Joe! Don't do it!"

Everyone looked at him.

"What did you say?" Joe asked.

Colin swallowed hard. "Nothing. Forget it."

Joe turned to Phil. "Well, come on, then. We have just enough time to get to the chemical place and back before chemistry class starts."

Joe and Phil hurried away.

When Frank turned back to Colin, Colin had disappeared.

"Where did he go?" Frank muttered. He suddenly felt very anxious and wasn't sure why, but he knew it had something to do with Colin Randles.

Frank hurried to the end of the hall, but Colin was nowhere in sight. Frank tried the restroom. He found Colin inside, washing his face with cold water.

"Colin! You have to tell me!" Frank said. "What did you mean when you told Joe not to go with Phil?"

Colin looked up. The water on his face made him look as though he had just come in from a thunderstorm.

"I saw a bad car wreck," Colin managed to say. "I don't think Joe and Phil will make it back here alive."

5 Mr. Hardy's Secret

Frank suddenly grabbed Colin's arm and said, "Come on—help me look for Phil's red sports car."

Frank dragged Colin down the hall. At the end he turned down a hallway that led to the parking lot next to the coach's office where Frank had parked the van.

"I can't miss class, Frank," Colin protested. "We're having a test, and I need to get a good grade."

Frank didn't let go. "Which class is it?" he asked.

"Speech," Colin replied. "I'm giving my major speech today."

"Is it Thompson's class?" Frank said.

Colin nodded.

"Don't worry, then. I'll make it right for you,"

Frank said. "Joe and I solved a mystery for her last year. She'd want you to help save my brother."

"I don't know if I can or not," Colin pleaded. "You can't just turn this stuff off and on."

They had reached the exit. Frank stopped and got in Colin's face.

"No more games, Colin. On our way to make sure Joe and Phil aren't killed in an accident, you're going to tell me everything!"

Frank didn't wait for Colin to reply. He pulled him out the door. The van was right by the exit, in a faculty parking place that the coach had allowed Frank to park in today.

Frank opened the passenger door and pushed Colin inside. He got in on the driver's side and squealed out of the parking lot.

"Where to?" Frank demanded. He was doing forty-five in a twenty-five mph zone. "Do we turn right or left up here?"

When Colin didn't say anything, Frank yelled. "Right or left?" To himself, he thought, *Get a hold of yourself, Hardy. This guy's making you crazy. You're totally losing it.*

"Don't you know the way to the chemical supply company?" Colin said. "I just moved here. I don't know my way around."

"There are a few chemical supply companies in Bayport," Frank said. "Joe didn't mention this one's name. Hurry! Think!"

"Left!" Colin shouted just as they reached the boulevard in front of Bayport High School.

Frank made a quick left, almost colliding with another car.

"Keep talking, Colin," Frank said.

"Sometimes what I see is in the future, Frank," Colin explained. "The wreck might not even happen today. It might happen next week or even next month."

Frank looked over at Colin. "I don't believe you. You seemed pretty certain before of when the crash was going to happen. I think you're just stalling."

"I'm not, I'm not," Colin said. "The image was very vivid, though, which usually means it's going to happen pretty soon."

"Then you'd better start seeing whatever it is you see, Colin," Frank warned him, "because if anything happens to Phil and Joe, I'll . . ."

"Make a right at the next intersection," Colin said. "The images are coming fast now." He gave Frank a wan smile. "Sometimes a lot of stress will do that."

Frank grinned himself. "Sorry. You're making me crazy. I don't understand any of this stuff."

"Neither do I," Colin admitted, "and I'm the psychic one."

Frank was driving twice the speed limit. If they were stopped, he only hoped it was by a police officer who recognized the Hardy name.

"There's a red sports car up ahead!" Colin shouted.

Frank could see Phil weaving in and out of traffic. He laid down on his horn. He pressed three longs, two shorts, and then one more long. Now, it was all up to Joe.

Frank saw Joe turn in their direction.

Frank signaled with the horn again. "We made up this horn code years ago, in case we ever needed it," he told Colin. He shook his head, thinking about the reason. "We decided that if either one of us were being kidnapped, the other would follow in a car, using this horn code, so that whoever was being kidnapped would know somebody was coming to the rescue."

Phil had pulled over to the side of the road, just at the edge of the next intersection. Frank maneuvered into the far lane so that he could pull up behind him.

Just then, they heard a loud blast of a horn. Beyond them, in the intersection, a runaway truck was barreling through at breakneck speed.

"That's it, Colin! That's what you saw!" Frank shouted. "Joe and Phil would have been smashed like a tin can if they hadn't stopped."

Frank jumped out of the van and ran up to Phil's sports car. Colin was right behind him.

"Hey, man, did you see that?" Phil said. "I'm glad you stopped us, Frank. We'd be long gone if you hadn't."

Frank could tell that Joe was visibly shaken. Suddenly, he gave Colin a hard stare.

Colin returned his look. "It's okay now, Joe. There won't be any more trouble," he said. "You guys can go on and get the chemicals. I'll talk to you later." He turned to Frank. "We need to get back to school. I have a speech to give."

Frank nodded. "I'll explain later, Joe. You might not believe me anyway."

Phil was giving all of them funny looks. "You guys are talking in code," he said. "Would you mind translating?"

"I'm not quite sure I have all of the pieces of the puzzle," Joe said, "but I'm getting there." He never took his eyes off Colin. "You're right. We'll talk more about this later." He turned to Phil. "We need to pick up those chemicals and get back to school."

The light had just turned green, so Phil put his car in gear and sped through the intersection. He waved without turning around. Joe stared straight ahead.

When they got back to school, Frank once again offered to explain to Mrs. Thompson why Colin was late, but Colin said he'd take care of it. Frank decided not to push it.

"Okay. Then I'll pick you up after school," Frank said. "We have to talk this thing out. Joe will be expecting you, too."

Colin sighed. "Okay," he said heavily. "It follows me everywhere I go. There's no getting away from it."

With that, he disappeared inside the building.

True to his word, Colin was waiting for them when Frank and Joe came out of the locker room. He followed them quietly to their van.

In fact, nobody said anything during the drive home. It was only when they pulled into the Hardys' driveway that Colin said, "I know what's going to happen now. We'll have to leave Bayport, just like we had to leave every other place we lived. It's always my fault."

Mrs. Hardy had some snacks ready for them, which meant that dinner was going to be served later than usual.

"Thanks, Mom!" the boys said. They introduced Colin to her.

"It's a pleasure, Colin," Mrs. Hardy said. "I hope you're getting used to Bayport. We've lived here a long time. It's a very interesting town."

"Oh, yes, I am," Colin said. "It's a *very* interesting town, all right."

Frank and Joe grabbed the snacks, pulled three soft-drink cans out of the fridge, and they led Colin to their room.

When they got there, Joe shut the door and immediately said, "So, earlier this afternoon, you saw us being killed, didn't you?" There was anger in his voice.

"Calm down, Joe," Frank said. "Colin and I have already had this conversation."

Frank flopped down on the floor and started eating a sandwich.

Joe and Colin stood facing each other for a few minutes, then they followed Frank's lead and joined him on the floor. They managed to put away several of the small sandwiches Mrs. Hardy had made.

Finally, Joe sighed and said, "Well, what made you change your mind, Colin? What made you decide to save me?"

"I didn't have a choice," Colin said.

"I made him," Frank explained.

Joe turned to Colin. "So if my brother hadn't made you find us, I'd be dead now."

Colin threw down his sandwich and got in Joe's face. "Am I supposed to save the world, Joe Hardy? Is that what you're saying?"

Joe didn't back down. He got right in Colin's face, too. "I'm not talking about saving the world, Randles, I'm talking about saving me."

"Well, I'm talking about saving the world," Colin countered. "Do you think yours is the only death I see every day?"

Joe blinked.

Frank stopped eating. "What do you mean?" he asked.

"I mean just what I said. I get these horrible visions every day. I see all of these awful things happening," Colin said. "Of course, I don't have any idea who most of these people are, they're just people, all over the world, who are . . ." He stopped and put his head in his hands. After a couple of seconds, he looked up. "I don't have any control over it. I have never had any control over it. The rest of my family is psychic, but I'm the most psychic, and I'm the one who gets my family in trouble. People don't want to know about the horrible things I see."

After a while, Joe said, "I'm sorry, Colin. I had no right to condemn you. It's just that I . . ."

Colin managed to grin. "It's just that you'd like to stick around for a few more years," he said. "I understand that perfectly."

After a brief pause Joe said, "You can't just let all those horrible things continue to happen. If you can stop them, then I think you have a responsibility to do just that."

Colin took a deep breath and let it out. "You're not telling me anything that I don't already feel, Joe, but you and Frank are the first people who've made me feel that this psychic thing is more gift than curse. I've been trying to push these visions out of my head for years."

Frank shook his head. "It's amazing," he said. "You study and study and study and you think you're so smart, because you know all of these facts, and what's really crazy is that we have just barely scratched the surface of all there is to know."

"People don't want to hear what I know," Colin said. "It scares them."

"The unknown scares people," Frank said. "That's just a fact we all have to accept."

"They don't want to believe," Colin added.

"Well, do you blame them?" Joe said. "It's kind of scary."

"I like the way Dad puts it," Frank said. "When people ask him if he believes something, he simply says that if he can't prove it or disprove it, then he just says so. He never says he doesn't believe something."

"Your father sounds like a very smart guy," Colin said.

"He is. He's a world-famous detective," Joe said. "He used to be with the New York Police Department. Now he works for himself."

"I'd like to meet him sometime," Colin said.

Frank cocked his ear toward the front of the house. "That should be him now," he said. "I think he'd like to meet you, too. Why don't you call your parents and ask them if you can stay for dinner?"

Joe laughed. "They may think we're a bad influence, after what happened at Callie's house," he said. "Be sure and tell them that we're not planning to play another practical joke on anybody."

"Shouldn't you ask your mom first?" Colin said.

"You're here. It's almost time for dinner," Joe said. "She already expects you to stay."

"There's a phone under Joe's pillow," Frank said. "He was on with Iola until late last night."

"Is she your girlfriend?" Colin asked.

"Yeah. We've been together for a while," Joe admitted. "She's great. We can talk to each other about almost anything."

Colin sighed. "It must be nice to have somebody like that," he said. He stood up, brushed a couple of crumbs off his pants, and reached under Joe's pillow for the phone.

After several rings, the answering machine came on. Colin left a message, telling his parents that he was eating dinner with the Hardy boys and that no, they weren't planning on playing any practical jokes on anyone.

Frank and Joe laughed at this, both feeling the lessening of tension that had been in the room when they first arrived home from school.

"Whose are these?" Colin asked. He was pointing to some plaques on the wall and some trophies in the bookcase.

"Well, we told you that our father was a detective," Joe explained, "but we didn't tell you that we had solved a few big cases ourselves." He stood up and walked over to where Colin was standing. "We got this airplane-shaped trophy when we solved a mystery at the airport," he said. "And we got this car-shaped trophy when we found out who was stealing all of the cars out on Shore Road."

"I'm impressed," Colin said.

"Well, I guess we all have our talents," Frank said, now standing up himself, "but I have to tell you that I've never seen anyone with talents like yours."

"Everyone has the potential to be a psychic," Colin said. "It just takes a little practice to develop your psychic abilities."

Joe and Frank stared at him.

"You mean I could do the same things that you do?" Joe said.

"No, I'm not saying that," Colin said. "I'm just saying that you can develop whatever psychic ability you do have. It's different in different people."

"Could you help us develop ours?" Frank asked.

Colin nodded. "If you're sure that's what you want to do."

Before either one of the Hardy boys could respond, there was a knock at the door.

"Come in," Frank called.

The door opened, and Fenton Hardy appeared. "Your mother said you had company," he said.

"Dad, this is Colin Randles," Joe said. "He and his family just moved here."

Colin walked over to Mr. Hardy and reached out his right hand to shake. He suddenly withdrew it, though, as if he had gotten an electric shock—and he started trembling uncontrollably.

"Colin!" Joe called.

Frank grabbed Colin and pulled him to a chair. Colin was breathing so hard that Frank thought he was going to hyperventilate.

Mr. Hardy hadn't moved from where he was standing.

"We'll explain in just a minute, Dad," Joe called from the bathroom. He was getting Colin a glass of water.

"Explain what?" Mr. Hardy said. "Do you think we need to call an ambulance?"

Colin suddenly groaned and opened his eyes. He looked around the room.

"Are you all right, Colin?" Mr. Hardy asked.

"It's nothing. It's nothing," Colin said. "Something just made me dizzy."

"Colin, don't do this!" Joe said. "You have to deal with it! What did you see?"

Colin swallowed hard, took a deep breath, and turned toward Mr. Hardy. "Okay. The man you're looking for lives in an apartment building at the corner of Jones Street and West Fourth Street in Greenwich Village in New York City. He'll be at the Jefferson Market Library two days from today, at two o'clock in the afternoon, and he'll have the secret documents with him. That's when he's supposed to give them to his contact. You can catch him then."

Joe and Frank Hardy had never seen such a stunned look on their father's face.

"What's he talking about, Dad?" Frank finally asked.

"One of my contacts with the government called me today. They're looking for a spy. They needed my help," Fenton Hardy said. "Colin just solved the mystery for me."

6 Kidnapped

A still-stunned Fenton Hardy herded all three of the boys into his study and closed the door. He told Mrs. Hardy and Aunt Gertrude that dinner was to be held up, and that they weren't to be disturbed under any circumstances.

Rarely did Frank and Joe see their father in such a serious mood. It was little unsettling for both of them, but then so was the revelation that he had been working on a secret case for the government that Colin Randles had just solved for him.

"This is getting weirder and weirder," Joe whispered to Frank, and Frank nodded his agreement.

As the boys seated themselves in chairs in front of Mr. Hardy's desk, Mr. Hardy made a telephone call. For several minutes he spoke in low tones, then he turned on the speaker phone.

"I can't tell you to whom you're talking, but I assure you, you'd recognize the name," Mr. Hardy said. He turned to Colin. "I want you to tell this person exactly what you told me just a few minutes ago."

Colin took at deep breath.

Frank and Joe could tell that he was extremely nervous.

"I'm . . . I'm not sure I can remember, well, exactly what I said," Colin said. He was rubbing the palms of his hands on the legs of his pants. "When these things happen, they happen so fast, and it's almost as if somebody else is talking for me. I'll try."

"That's all we can ask," Fenton said.

Colin began. When he hesitated, Frank and Joe prompted him. When Colin finished, Frank and Joe agreed with their father that Colin had repeated everything that he had first said to Mr. Hardy.

The voice on the telephone asked Mr. Hardy to turn off the speaker, which Mr. Hardy did.

Fenton Hardy listened to the person for several more minutes, uttered a few low agreements, then hung up.

"Colin, there's no way you could have known anything about this case, in the normal way," Mr. Hardy said, "but you've solved it. Government agents will take over from here." He looked at Frank and Joe. "Does this have anything to do with the questions you were asking me about psychic detectives the other night?"

"Well, sort of, Dad," Joe said.

For the next few minutes, the three boys told Mr. Hardy everything that had happened over the last few days.

Mr. Hardy listened carefully, never passing judgment. When he heard about the practical joke during the séance, he frowned, but both Frank and Joe knew that he liked Chet Morton and wouldn't really think any less of him.

Finally, Mr. Hardy said, "Nothing said during these last few minutes must leave this room, boys . . . agreed?"

Frank and Joe nodded. They were used to hearing things in confidence from their father.

Colin nodded, too. "I understand, Mr. Hardy. I don't like to let many people know about my psychic abilities. Very few of them understand."

"I've been involved with several criminal cases where psychics have given us the last bit of information we needed to solve the crime," Fenton Hardy said. "I've found most of them don't want publicity. They just want to help."

"That's the way I feel, too, sir," Colin said.

Mr. Hardy stood up. "Well, I don't know about you boys, but I'm starved. How about some dinner?"

"Sounds great," Joe said. "I barely had anything to eat after school."

After dinner, the boys went back to Joe and Frank's room.

"When do we start?" Joe said.

Colin looked puzzled. "Start?"

"Yeah! Start!" Joe reminded him. "I want to find out how psychic I am!"

Colin shrugged and looked at his watch. "We can start now, if you want to. I don't have any homework." He turned to Frank. "I think I aced my speech. I was the last name on the list, so I didn't miss giving it, and Mrs. Thompson accepted my explanation. The Hardy name really opens doors around here."

"I've got a little homework, but I can spare some time for this," Frank said. "I'm as interested as Joe in finding out more about what psychics do."

Colin made himself comfortable on the floor. "Most people start with psychic readings," he said. "Some people call it fortune-telling."

"That sounds like a good place to start," Joe said. "I'd love to be able to tell fortunes."

"Isn't that fake?" Frank asked.

"Psychic readings aren't fake," Colin said, "but sometimes there are false psychics who do perform them." He shrugged. "You've got phoneys in everything. The world of the psychic is no different."

"That's true," Joe said.

For the next several minutes, Colin told them

what they needed to do a psychic reading.

He said they were probably receiving messages from someone when they said that a person gave off good vibes or when they talked about having a lucky hunch.

"You're not reading someone's mind," Colin explained, "you're reading their energy."

Colin told them they had to relax. They couldn't rush psychic readings. They had to allow themselves to receive the information from another person.

Frank and Joe followed Colin's instructions.

Suddenly, Joe jumped up and went to the door. "What?" he yelled down the hallway.

At that moment, Mrs. Hardy appeared. "Well, you must have read my mind, Joe, because I just remembered that I needed to tell you something."

Joe blinked and turned around to face a grinning Frank and Colin.

Colin shrugged.

"I guess I did, Mom," Joe said. "What did you forget to tell me?"

"They called today to tell you that the CDs you ordered are in," Mrs. Hardy said. "They'll only hold them for you for a week."

"Okay, Mom," Joe said. "Thanks."

When Mrs. Hardy was gone, Joe said, "That's amazing. I knew she was coming to our room to tell me something."

"It works, Joe," Colin said. "It really does." He

looked at his watch. "I need to be going. Could I bum a ride home?"

"Yeah—we can pick up my CDs on the way," Joe said.

Frank grabbed the keys to the van. After Colin went to the kitchen and thanked Mrs. Hardy for dinner, the three of them headed outside.

"I don't think your aunt likes me," Colin said.

"What did she say to you to make you think that?" Joe asked.

"She didn't say anything." Colin said. "She just had a frown on her face when I was thanking your mother for dinner."

"She does the same thing to us, Colin. Don't think anything about it," Frank said. "Aunt Gertrude just has a 'distinct' personality, that's all."

CD City was on the way to Colin's house. Frank pulled into the parking lot, let Joe run in and get his CDs—which only took a few minutes—and then they pulled back out onto the boulevard.

Colin was quiet all the way. He seemed to have sunk into a really dark mood.

If all psychics are this moody, Joe thought, *I don't think I want to develop any psychic abilities I might have. I'd just as soon not know all of this stuff.*

When they reached the Randles' house, Colin jumped out. Without looking back, he said, "Thanks, guys! I'll see you tomorrow." In an instant, he had disappeared into his house.

"Do you think he'll be all right?" Joe asked.

Frank shrugged. "Who knows?" He backed out of the Randles' driveway and headed home. "There's no telling what's really going on in his mind, Joe. And I'm not sure I really want to know."

"I know what you mean," Joe said. "I know what you mean."

When the Hardy boys saw Colin the next morning, he seemed to be in an even darker mood than he was the night before.

"What's wrong, Colin?" Frank asked when they got to English class.

"Today's the day," Colin whispered to Frank.

Frank frowned his puzzlement. Colin looked around to see if anyone else was paying attention to them, and when he found no one was, he added, "I've been feeling it even more strongly, Frank. I know now that it's a girl. She's not who she thinks she is."

"I know you said that, Colin, but I can't think of anyone it might be," Frank said. "I know everybody in this school—well, maybe not everyone all that well, because there are a bunch of new kids this year—but I really do think they are who they say they are."

"That's the point, Frank," Colin explained. "She thinks she knows who she is, but she doesn't."

This conversation is getting too weird, Frank

54

decided. He wanted to be friends with Colin, but already some of the other guys were keeping their distance. He didn't think that was fair, but he could certainly understand.

Frank was glad when Ms. Long said that today she was just going to talk to them about British poets. He didn't particularly like British poets, but at least he wouldn't have to do group work with Colin. Frankly, he wasn't sure Colin would be able to do any group work. Frank wished that whatever was bothering Colin would surface fully, so that the problem could be solved.

It didn't take long.

As they headed out of English class, Colin bumped into Melanie Johnson.

"It's you!" Colin cried. "It's you!"

Melanie stood, mouth open, staring at Colin.

All of the students in the vicinity stopped to stare, too. Most of them knew just enough about Colin to think that he was a little bit "off," and now he was showing them that they were right.

Frank grabbed Colin by the arm and tried to pull him away from the gathering crowd.

"No, Frank, no!" Colin said. "She's not who she thinks she is!"

Melanie had had enough time to recover and was shaking her head in disbelief.

Frank didn't know Melanie Johnson well, but he knew a lot about her. While he didn't dislike her, he didn't particularly like her, either. Her family was one of the wealthiest in Bayport. If Melanie had wanted to, she could have attended boarding school in Europe, but she preferred to stay in Bayport for high school during the week, and party in New York City on the weekends.

"Who is this creep, Frank?" Melanie said. "A friend of yours?"

Colin was staring at Melanie. "I know what I'm talking about. You're not totally who you think you are!"

"Oh, really?" Melanie said. "Well, who am I?"

"You're—"

"What's going on here?"

Oh, great! Frank thought.

Mr. Brooks, one of the assistant principals, had made his way through the crowd. When he saw Colin, he rolled his eyes. "Are you having a problem here, Mr. Randles?"

"He's not having a problem, Mr. Brooks," Frank said. "It was just a misunderstanding."

"This creep was insulting me, Mr. Brooks," Melanie said. "I think I need to call my father and report him."

Frank saw Mr. Brooks blanch. Not only did the Johnson family give thousands to the Bayport public schools, but Mr. Johnson was on the school board. It wouldn't do to have him mad about anything.

"There's no need to do that, Melanie," Mr. Brooks said. "I can take care of this."

"Well, just see that you do," Melanie said. She tossed her long blond hair and headed down the hall, followed by her entourage of hangers-on.

Joe had now joined Frank. "What was that all about?" he said under his breath.

Frank could only roll his eyes and shake his head.

Mr. Brooks was staring at Colin. Frank was sure that the assistant principal wanted to expel Colin right then and there.

"I want you in my office right now, Colin Randles," Mr. Brooks said. Turning to Frank and Joe, he added, "And I think the Hardy boys need to come too."

The three of them followed Mr. Brooks down the hall toward the administrative office complex. Several students gawked at them, knowing full well what was to come.

As they stepped into Mr. Brooks's outer office, Mr. Brooks looked over at his secretary and said, "I don't want to be disturbed."

Joe felt like telling him that he was already disturbed enough, but he knew that wouldn't be wise. Mr. Brooks was trying to earn a reputation as a hard-nosed administrator, and he was doing a really good job of it so far.

Inside his office, Mr. Brooks said, "Sit."

There were only two chairs in front of his desk, so Frank remained standing.

Mr. Brooks took a deep breath, released it, looked straight at Colin and said, "I want to know why you were harassing Melanie Johnson."

Colin returned his look. "I wasn't harassing her. I was trying to tell her something."

"What were you trying to tell her?" Mr. Brooks demanded.

Colin leaned closer to Mr. Brooks. "I was trying to tell her that she was kidnapped when she was two years old!"

7 Colin Is in Danger

Mr. Brooks was so angry about what Colin had just said that he was turning purple. In fact, he looked like he was going to choke to death.

Joe glanced over at Frank and knew he was thinking the same thing. Should they try to perform CPR on the assistant principal?

Just then, a gurgling sound came out of Mr. Brooks's throat, and his color began to return to normal.

"You're nuts! You're totally nuts, Randles," Mr. Brooks managed to say. "You should be locked up somewhere."

"I don't think you're supposed to say things like that to students, Mr. Brooks," Joe said. "It could probably get you in trouble."

Frank rolled his eyes at Joe. He agreed with his brother, but he also didn't think this was the time or place to suggest that someone be politically correct.

Fortunately, Mr. Brooks either wasn't paying attention or chose to ignore Joe's comment, because he didn't take his eyes off Colin.

"I know all about your family, Randles, about how they're *psychic* and everything," Mr. Brooks continued. The way he said "psychic" made it sound like a dirty word. "It was people like you and your family who caused problems for me and my family. This . . . *psychic* took my poor mother for almost every cent we had, telling her all kinds of things, promising her that she'd be rich, if she kept coming to the readings." Here he took a deep breath, let it out, and through gritted teeth added, "I despise people like you!"

Wow! Frank thought. *Does this man have an agenda or what?*

Joe was amazed at how Colin simply sat there and listened, not showing any emotion whatsoever. *He's probably heard this all before,* Joe thought.

The bell rang to start the next class.

"As you know, Mr. Brooks, Colin's new in town—and this was all just a big misunderstanding," Frank said. "You shouldn't take out your frustrations on him. Why don't you just let us go on to class and we'll make sure this doesn't happen again?"

Mr. Brooks turned to him. Frank felt like the

man was seeing him for the first time. "What?"

Frank repeated what he had said. He could tell that Mr. Brooks wanted to lash out at him, too, but seemed to realize that he had gone too far in what he had said to Colin. He looked like he was weighing his options.

Mr. Brooks picked up a pad and started writing. He handed each of the boys a slip of paper. "Tardy passes," he said. "And if this happens again . . . well, just make sure it doesn't." He opened a file on his desk and started reading it.

Frank motioned for Colin and Joe to follow him out. He didn't want to give Mr. Brooks a chance to rethink his decision.

When they got back to the hall, Joe let out a big sigh. "Wow! I hope that guy finds another job and fast. I can't imagine having to deal with him again."

"Assistant principals don't stay for more than one year. They're really just principals in training," Frank said. "Sometimes prisons hire teachers to teach the inmates. Let's hope one of those jobs opens up soon. Brooks would be perfect for it."

They boys separated to go to their individual classes, but they agreed to meet after school to go to the Hardys' house to talk.

On the ride home, Colin was quiet as usual. Frank and Joe were busy thinking about what had happened earlier, so they weren't talking much either.

Mrs. Hardy had a big plate of cookies and cold milk ready for them. They took everything into Joe and Frank's room and shut the door. After they had each eaten a few cookies, Frank said, "Okay, Colin, first let me tell you that I believe what you said about Melanie Johnson—even if it does sound really wild."

"I do, too, Colin," Joe added, "but you really can't go around accosting people like that, if you want to live a normal life here in Bayport."

Colin grinned. "I know. I know. It's just that I've had this really dark feeling ever since we've been in Bayport about *someone*. When I bumped into Melanie in the hall today, I knew immediately she was the person I 'saw' things happening to when she was just two or three."

Frank shook his head. "Colin, you have to understand how hard this is for people to accept," he said. "As far as I'm concerned, you've proven yourself, but from here on out, you just have to be careful how you handle the information you receive."

Colin nodded. "I know."

Joe looked over at Frank. "What are we going to do about this?" he said. "We can't just forget it."

"I know," Frank said. "And I've been thinking about it all afternoon."

"Well?" Joe said.

"We're going to start investigating," Frank replied. "Is that what you wanted to hear?"

"That's what I was planning to do," Joe said. "And I was hoping you'd be up for it."

Frank looked at Colin. "We need to know everything that you've seen about Melanie," he said. "Don't leave out any details."

Colin took a deep breath and closed his eyes. "The first day we were in Bayport, I got this really heavy feeling. I don't know how else to describe it. I also got a terrible headache and started receiving images—well, really they were like blinding flashes—of a little girl. She wasn't more than two or three years old, and this man was carrying her out of a house. She was crying, and calling for her mother."

"What else do you remember about the little girl?" Joe asked.

"She was holding a little stuffed lamb." Colin hesitated for a moment. "I think the man had to go back for it. I don't think the little girl had it at first. I think the man went back for it to stop her from crying so much."

"That's strange," Frank said. "Kidnappers won't usually do things like that."

"No," Joe agreed. "They snatch a kid and are out of the place as fast as possible."

"Anything else?" Frank said.

"That's it." Colin leaned his head back against the edge of Joe's bed. "I might have been able to receive more images, but I kept trying to block them."

"That's too bad," Joe said. "We need all the clues we can get."

"I didn't want to cause my family any more trouble, but I haven't been too successful at blocking all the images," Colin said. "Sometimes the visions are just too strong to keep out of my head."

"What does that mean?" Joe asked.

"It usually means that whoever I'm getting them from is under a lot of stress," Colin replied.

Frank frowned. "Well, if Melanie is sending them, she sure didn't look like she was under a lot of stress today."

"She may not be the only one," Colin said. "Whoever kidnapped her may be *thinking* about what happened and I may be receiving both their thoughts. That's what could be making the signals so strong."

"You mean Melanie and whoever kidnapped her are psychic?" Joe asked.

Colin shook his head. "You don't have to be psychic to *think,* Joe," he said. "We can all think. But you do have to have a well-developed psychic ability to *receive* the messages. I was born that way. And, like I said, people can develop their psychic abilities over a period of time."

"Well, I'm not having much luck," Joe said. "I haven't received any messages since yesterday when Mom was thinking about the CDs I ordered."

"I'm not having much luck, either," Frank added. He didn't say that he wasn't quite sure he wanted to be psychic. Truly, if it meant dealing with what Colin had to deal with on a daily basis, he'd turn it down. "But that's not solving this mystery."

"Should we tell Dad?" Joe asked.

Frank shook his head. "We'll keep it among the three of us for the time being," he said. "We need to figure out a plan of action first. We also need to decide why we're really doing this."

"I can tell you why," Colin interjected. "Melanie didn't want to leave. The man was taking her by force."

No one said anything for several minutes. The three of them continued to eat cookies and think about how they wanted to proceed.

Finally Frank said, "From what I've heard, Melanie Johnson is never at home in the evenings. She's always at a party or at the movies or just driving around. I think Joe and I should follow her and see if we can pick up some clues."

"I'll come along," Colin said.

"I don't think that's a good idea," Frank said. "You're not exactly the most popular person at Bayport High School now."

"If Melanie saw you with us, she'd really be suspicious," Joe added. "As it is, we'll still have to make sure she doesn't spot us."

Colin reluctantly agreed. "What I can do, though," he added, "is to stop blocking the messages I've been receiving about Melanie."

"That would be good," Joe said. "We'll need every bit of information we can put together to solve this mystery."

Joe had some homework he had to get started on, so Frank drove Colin home. He got back just in time for dinner.

Neither one of the boys felt like talking much at the table, but Aunt Gertrude seemed interested in what was happening to Nella and Colin.

"What do the kids at school think about them?" she asked. "Do they make fun of their psychic abilities?"

"Sometimes," Joe mumbled. He took a big bite of mashed potatoes to keep from having to explain.

"Figures," Aunt Gertrude said, more to herself than to anyone else. "I'll never understand people who don't keep open minds."

Frank looked over at Joe. They were thinking the same thing—that that sounded strange coming from Aunt Gertrude. She was one of the most opinionated people they knew.

Through the rest of dinner, Aunt Gertrude complained about how hard Fenton was working, that he was away from home too much, that he should spend more time in the yard, and that he had promised to fix the window in her bedroom, and he still hadn't done that.

Finally, Frank and Joe had a chance to excuse themselves and go to their room. Joe finished up his homework, and Frank searched the Internet for information for a project in one of his classes.

Joe looked at his watch. "It's six-thirty, Frank. If we're going to follow Melanie tonight, we'd better leave. She's probably finishing dinner about now."

Frank shut down the computer, and Joe shouted to Mrs. Hardy that they were going out for a while.

Melanie Johnson lived in a part of Bayport that had million-dollar homes. It also had several busy streets that crisscrossed the area, so the Hardys knew they wouldn't be stopped—if they didn't act too suspicious.

When they got to Melanie's house, they found several cars parked along the curb in front.

"She may be having a party," Joe said. "She may not be going anywhere tonight."

Frank pulled the van in behind an SUV and turned off the engine and the headlights.

"Or some of her friends could have met here, with plans to go somewhere else, all in one car," Frank said.

"Let's hope," Joe said.

After a few minutes, several girls came out of a gate that led to the back of the Johnsons' house. They were laughing about something as they headed down the driveway toward one of the vehicles parked in front.

"Duck!" Frank said to Joe.

The boys ducked just in time. The vehicle the

girls all piled into was the SUV that was parked in front of the van. Frank hoped he hadn't parked so close that the driver couldn't get out.

The girls must have rolled down the windows of the SUV, because Frank and Joe heard someone mention Colin's name, which was followed by hysterical laughter.

Whoever was driving ended up bumping the front fender of the van, but Frank didn't think it was enough to cause any damage, so he decided not to get out and examine it. He knew he would have a lot of explaining to do.

The SUV headed down the street at a relatively fast pace. Frank started the van and pulled out after it.

"I think we can stay pretty close to them," Frank said. "Being tailed is the last thing they'll be thinking about."

Joe laughed.

The traffic was relatively light, and the SUV had big taillights, so it was easy to keep the girls in sight.

"I wonder where we're going," Joe said.

"Who knows?" Frank said.

They didn't have to wait long for an answer. The SUV pulled into the parking lot of a multiplex theater. All of the girls piled out and headed up to the box office.

"I hope it's something I want to see," Frank said.

"If it's a romance, I may just stay in the lobby and eat popcorn," Joe said.

"I don't think so. We need to sit as close to them as possible and listen to what they say," Frank said. "You can ignore what's on the screen."

As it turned out, the movie Melanie and her friends bought tickets for was a comedy that both the Hardy boys had been wanting to see.

"Even if we don't find out anything tonight," Joe said, "it won't be a total waste of time."

Frank bought their tickets. He and Joe held back from going into the theater while Melanie and her friends nearly bought out the concession stand and went into the theater.

The movie was scheduled to start in a couple of minutes. Frank suggested they wait to enter until the movie started, so it would be dark.

"Uh-oh," Joe whispered. "There's Chief Collig and his wife." Ezra Collig was the chief of the Bayport Police Department and a friend of the Hardys. "If he sees us, he'll want to know if we're working on a case, and may give us away."

They weren't too far from the men's restroom, so they ducked inside and both headed to separate stalls. After several minutes, when they thought the Colligs had already gone into their movie, they slipped out and headed to their theater.

Inside, the previews were just starting. Frank and Joe stood at the back of the auditorium until their eyes had adjusted. The theater wasn't too crowded, but there were enough people that they wouldn't be too conspicuous.

"There they are, in the middle, and there are some seats behind them," Joe whispered.

Frank looked. They'd have to pass in front of some other people, but the middle seats would be perfect.

They made their way down the aisle until they reached the row behind the one where Melanie and her friends were sitting. They had to squeeze past many people, but they finally made it to their seats.

They sat down quietly, hoping that neither Melanie nor her friends would turn around and recognize their profiles.

They didn't. The girls were whispering to each other, giggling about what they had just said, and were totally ignoring what was on the screen.

Once, someone at the end of the Hardys' row made a loud shushing sound, but Melanie and her friends ignored it.

Joe was glad, because if they didn't stop whispering, maybe one of them would give the boys a clue that would help them solve their mystery.

Most of what the girls were whispering about was innocuous and silly, Joe thought, until right before the opening credits of the movie.

Melanie leaned over to the person next to her and said, "Don't worry. My boyfriend has plans for Colin Randles. He won't be bothering me anymore."

8 The Deserted Building

The Hardy boys jumped up from their seats.
They startled Melanie and her friends, but Frank
was sure they did not give away their identities.
The boys made their way back down through the
aisle, whispering "Excuse me" as fast as they
could.

As they hurried toward the exit, Joe said, "We
should have suspected something like that from
her, Frank."

"I guess, but we really don't know her that well,
Joe," Frank said. "She's in the really rich set, and
she normally keeps to herself."

"Well, we know now," Joe said.

They had reached the lobby and were running
toward the outside doors.

"Is there anything wrong?" a voice called. "Is there a problem with the projection?"

"It's okay!" Joe shouted. "We forgot to do our homework."

Several people in the lobby started laughing. Frank hoped that nobody recognized them.

Just as they stepped outside, a loud clap of thunder shook the area.

Frank looked up. "Oh, great!" he muttered. "Just what we need."

Flashes of lightning streaked across the sky, creating spiderweb-like patterns above Bayport.

"When that hits, we're going to get soaked," Joe said.

The Hardy boys jumped into the van and raced out of the parking lot.

"Where should we go first?" Joe asked.

"The Randles'," Frank replied. "We need to find out where Colin went tonight. That's probably where he met Melanie's boyfriend."

"Good idea," Joe agreed. "Maybe somebody there could give us a description of the guy." He looked over at Frank. "Do you think Melanie's boyfriend actually kidnapped Colin in broad daylight?"

Frank shook his head. "No. I think he probably said something that made Colin go with him willingly."

"I've got it," Joe said. "He probably told Colin that Melanie wanted to talk to him in private."

"That would have done it!" Frank said. "In fact, that might be the only thing that would make Colin go with someone he didn't know."

The street in front of the multiplex led the Hardys to another one of Bayport's main thoroughfares, which at this hour wasn't so crowded that they couldn't make good time. They missed a couple of lights, which slowed them down, but fifteen minutes later, they pulled up in front of the Randles' house.

"Good! Lights!" Joe said. "Somebody's at home."

More thunder and lightning greeted them as they ran up the walk to the Randles' front porch. Frank quickly rang the doorbell.

Joe stepped off the porch and scanned the sky. "Maybe the storm'll go around us," he said. "Most of the heavy stuff seems to be over toward the west."

"Let's hope so," Frank said. He rang the doorbell again.

When nobody had answered after several minutes, Joe thought that maybe the lights had just been left on while the Randles had gone out for something. He said as much to Frank.

"I don't think so, Joe. The Randles don't have a lot of money," Frank said. "They'd remember to turn out the lights." Instead of ringing the bell again, Frank knocked as hard as he could.

That worked. In a few minutes, the porch light went on and Nella opened the door.

"Frank! Joe!" Nella said. She looked around. "Where's Colin?"

"That's what we were going to ask you, Nella," Joe said. "You mean he's not here?"

"No. I told him where you said to meet him, and that's where he went," Nella said. Suddenly, a frown appeared on her face. "That was you who called, wasn't it?"

Frank shook his head.

"Shoot!" Nella said. "I hope it's not happening again!"

"You hope what's not happening again?" Frank asked.

"Everywhere we've lived, there's been trouble, because of Colin's psychic visions," Nella explained. "I was hoping it wouldn't happen in Bayport."

"But this isn't your fault, Nella," Joe said.

"Oh, yes it is, Joe," Nella insisted. She opened the screen door. "Come in. We've got to think this out. We have to find Colin."

Joe followed Frank into the Randles' living room. It was clean, but the furniture was from the 1950s.

"Have a seat," Nella said. "Do you want something to drink?"

"No, we're fine, Nella," Frank said. "Let's just figure out something quick. Colin might be in danger." He looked around. "Are your parents here?"

"No. Mom and Dad have been working late, ever

since they got jobs at Mr. Shaw's hardware store," Nella said. "It was just Colin and me when you— uh, whoever it was—called."

Frank and Joe sat down together on the sofa, facing the chair that Nella had collapsed in.

"Start at the beginning," Frank said.

"Don't leave out anything," Joe added.

"The phone rang about five-thirty, and I answered it. It sounded just like you, Frank," Nella said. "You said you wanted Colin to meet you downtown, at . . ." Nella jumped up and ran over to a table where there was a telephone. She picked up a piece of paper. ". . . 2314 North March Street. You said you had followed Melanie Johnson there and had something really interesting to tell him."

"Colin went there?" Frank said.

Nella nodded. "You . . . uh, the caller, said one of the city buses stopped at that address, so Colin walked to the corner one block over and caught the bus downtown." She took a deep breath. "I had a feeling there was something about that call that wasn't right, but our parents have told us to suppress our psychic ability, so we won't keep getting into trouble. So I went with it."

"I guess this was one time when you should have paid attention to what you were feeling," Joe said.

Nella nodded.

"We've got to find Colin, Nella. The person who called was Melanie Johnson's boyfriend," Frank

76

said. "We followed Melanie and some of her friends to a movie tonight. We overheard her telling them that her boyfriend had plans for Colin."

Nella gasped. "Oh, Frank! Joe!" she cried. "I have to go with you. I can't just stay here and do nothing."

Frank shook his head. "We'll take you to Callie's house, though. I don't want you staying here. I don't know this crowd very well, but I do know they play rough, and they might not want to stop with Colin."

Joe called Callie on his cell phone and told her they were on their way over with Nella.

Outside, it had started to rain lightly. "Well, we didn't luck out entirely," Joe said, once more scanning the sky, "but I think we'll miss the really heavy rain."

"That's good," Frank said. He didn't have to add that it would be harder to find Colin in weather like this.

When they reached Callie's house, Callie was waiting outside for them, under an umbrella. Frank only stopped long enough to let Nella out, and then they headed on downtown.

When they exited onto the street that would lead them to the address on March Street, Joe said, "I have a feeling this is going to be a wild goose chase, Frank. I don't think Melanie's boyfriend will still be there."

"No, he won't, but Colin might," Frank said, "but

there's no telling what condition we'll find him in."

Joe hadn't thought about that.

The downtown area was mostly deserted at that hour, because of the rain and because the new shopping centers on the outskirts of town had taken away a lot of business. There was an urban renewal plan to rebuild downtown Bayport, but it was still in the beginning stages of development. If it ever happened, the area would be hopping again.

"There's 2314," Joe said. "It's an abandoned building."

"Figures," Frank said. "We still need to check it out and see if we can find anything."

They parked the van directly across the street, got out, and, ignoring the drizzle, crossed to 2314. Halfway there, Joe remembered the flashlight they kept in the van, so he went back for it and then rejoined Frank, who was now waiting for him on the sidewalk in front of the building.

The streetlights didn't give off much light, but the boys could see that the front door was padlocked. Above the address, Joe saw a date cut into stone: 1927. "This is a really old building," he said.

"I think it's one they're planning to turn into expensive apartments," Frank said. "They're hoping to save most of the original buildings down here."

Joe wasn't sure he'd want to live in an apartment in this part of Bayport, unless there were other things going on downtown, too. Of course, he had heard there were plans for lots of restaurants and stores and movie theaters, so it might not be too bad. He'd wait and see.

Frank tried the door. It was locked. "Whoever called Colin obviously didn't use this building for anything," he said.

Joe looked around. "Do you think Melanie's boyfriend was standing just inside that alley over there until Colin got here?" he said. "He could have watched him get off the bus and then called him over."

"But if he thought you called, like Nella said, then why would he approach a stranger," Joe said, "especially with all that's happened to him in the last few days?"

"Think about it, Joe," Frank said. "It's dark over there. Melanie's boyfriend might look like me in the dark."

"You're right," Joe agreed. "If he can sound like you, he might have been able to fool Colin long enough to get him to the mouth of the alley."

"I say we check out the alley," Frank said. "Whoever was there might have left a clue of some kind. Maybe the rain hasn't washed away everything."

They soon reached the corner of the building. Joe switched on the flashlight, and they started walking slowly down the alley. The recent rain, mixed with all the trash that had collected, made for a very unpleasant smell, but they knew they couldn't worry about that now.

Joe shone the flashlight up and down the side of the building. Suddenly he stopped and shone the flashlight back toward the street.

"What's wrong?" Frank whispered.

"I just had the feeling that somebody was behind me, that's all," Joe said. He was suddenly thinking about what Colin had said about psychic readings. Was he receiving someone's messages? "Now I wish I'd spent some more time working on what Colin said we needed to do to develop our psychic senses," Joe said. "It might be easier to find him."

"I was thinking the same thing," Frank said.

Just then they heard a noise toward the back of the alley.

"Who's there?" Frank called. His voice echoed through the alley.

"Go away!" a voice said. It was weak, but it sounded like a man.

Frank and Joe looked at each other.

"It's okay," Joe called to the man. "We won't hurt you."

"That's what they all say," the man said. "They don't tell the truth."

"Well, we're telling the truth," Frank called. "We're looking for a friend of ours. We think he may be in trouble."

For a few minutes, the man said nothing more. Frank and Joe heard a shuffling sound, and a homeless person came out from behind one of the garbage bins into the light of the flashlight.

"If you'll give me some money, I'll tell you about your friend," the man said. The boys smelled alcohol on the man's breath.

"I can guess what he wants the money for," Joe whispered, "but we have to find out about Colin."

The man stayed where he was. Frank and Joe walked slowly toward him, looking behind them from time to time to make sure this wasn't some kind of a trap. They soon got to where the man was standing. The smell coming from him was even worse than the smell from the alley.

"Our friend thought he was meeting me here," Frank said, "but it was only someone who said he was me."

"We think he's in serious trouble," Joe added. "We have to find him."

"They beat him up. They did a pretty good job of it, too," the man said. "I saw them."

"Is he still here?" Joe said. He started shining the light all around the area.

The man held out his hand. "Where's my money?"

"You haven't given us the information we need," Frank said. "You don't get your money until you tell us where our friend is."

"He's not in the alley. He's in there." The man

pointed to the building at 2314 North March Street. "I saw them take him inside and beat him up."

"We tried the front door. It's locked," Frank said. "I don't think you're telling the truth."

"One of them had a key. He unlocked the front door," the man said. "But he locked it again when they left."

"What are we going to do now, Frank?" Joe said. "Colin's inside that building, hurt, and we can't get in."

"Yes, you can," the man said. He had his hand out for his money. "I know a way in that you don't need a key for."

9 Mr. Johnson's Wrath

After handing the man a few bills, Frank and Joe followed him to the top of the alley's T.

"There's an old service entrance back here. It's hidden behind a couple of Dumpsters," the man said. "It looks like it's boarded up, but it's easy to take the boards off and get inside."

"Does anybody else know about this entrance?" Joe asked. He didn't want to run into another homeless person who might not be as accommodating as their newfound friend.

"No, they don't," the man said. "This is my alley, and the other homeless people stay out of here."

"That's good to know," Frank said. "I mean, it's good to know that you have a place to call your own."

When they reached the service entrance, they

squeezed behind the Dumpsters. Joe shone the flashlight on the boards so that the man could see to remove the nails.

All of this was amazing to the Hardy boys. The door really did appear to be nailed shut, but with just a little tugging from the man, the nails came right out.

"I don't know what I'm going to do if they turn this place into apartments," the man said, as he continued to remove nails and to stack the boards neatly at the side of the entrance.

"I wouldn't worry too much about that," Frank said. "I think that's a long way off."

When all of the boards had been removed, the man gave the door a push. It creaked open.

The three of them stepped inside, and Joe shone the light around to help orient them.

"Now, where did you see them beating up our friend?" Frank asked. "This is a big building. It'd be hard to search through all of it."

"It's on the third floor. Follow me, but watch your step," the man said. "The wood in the place is rotten."

With the man in the lead and Joe's flashlight showing them the way, the three of them headed into the interior of the old building.

"What were you doing on the third floor?" Frank asked. He was suddenly beginning to get suspicious.

"I saw those two guys bringing your friend in

through the front entrance," the man said. "So I went in this back way to check it out. I wanted to know what they were doing in my building."

"Well, if they had a key, they may own it," Joe observed.

"That's what I thought. I wanted to know if they were going to do something that would force me to leave," the man said. "I thought I might overhear their conversation. Instead, I saw them beating up your friend."

Slowly, they twisted and turned down corridors that probably had once been bustling with the business of the residents of half a century or more ago.

"We have to take the stairs," the man said to them. "The elevators don't work."

The man started up the stairs, followed by Frank, with Joe and his flashlight bringing up the rear. Suddenly there was a cracking noise, and Frank yelped as his foot went through a rotten board.

Joe rushed to his brother and shone the flashlight on the step. Together, he and the man helped pull Frank's foot out of the hole.

Mindless of the dirt on the stairs, Frank sat down to rub his ankle.

"Did you twist it, Frank?" Joe asked.

"I don't think so," Frank replied. "It doesn't matter, though. We can't stop. We have to find Colin."

The three of them started back up the stairs. From time to time, the man would tell them which boards to step over. They were able to make it to the third floor without another accident.

This floor wasn't as cluttered as the ground floor, so it was easier to find their way along the corridors.

Finally they came to what looked like it used to be a complex of offices.

"Your friend's in there," the man whispered.

Slowly, Frank opened the door, and Joe shone the flashlight inside. There, lying on the dusty floor, curled up in the fetal position, was Colin Randles.

"I hope he's still alive," the man said.

"Colin!" Frank shouted.

The Hardy boys rushed to Colin's side.

Melanie's boyfriend and his friend had obviously used Colin's face as a punching bag. His eyes were swollen shut.

"Colin?" Joe said. "Can you hear me?"

Suddenly, Colin groaned and tried to bring his hands up to his face.

"No, don't move," Frank said. "It's Frank and Joe Hardy. You're going to be okay."

Frank turned around to ask the man something, but the man had disappeared.

"Oh, that's just great," Frank said. "Where did he go?"

"He probably got scared, Frank," Joe said. "He showed us where Colin was at least."

"Do you think the two of us can get him downstairs and out to the van?" Frank asked. "Can you hold the flashlight and his feet, too?"

"There's no other choice," Joe said. "It would take an ambulance a while to get here."

"You're right," Frank said. "We've got to handle this ourselves."

Frank grabbed Colin under the shoulders, while Joe, holding the flashlight in his right hand, picked up Colin's legs.

"I'm just glad he's not as big as Chet," Frank said, as they headed out of the office and into the corridor. "We'd never be able to do this."

With Joe leading the way, they made it to the stairs and started down.

"Let's stay as close to the banister as possible, Frank," Joe said. "That'll be something to grab if we step on a rotten board."

"Good idea. And the steps should be stronger at the edge," Frank reminded him. "It's usually in the middle that the board's rotten."

Joe thought it was going to take them forever, but they finally made it down to the first floor. They started toward the service entrance.

"I just thought of something, Frank," Joe said. "What if the man boarded up the door?"

"I was thinking the same thing," Frank said. "But a good shove should knock the boards down."

As it turned out, they didn't have to worry. The service entrance was still open.

"Our new friend is okay after all. He just didn't

want to be up there if an authority showed up, I guess," Frank said, "but he knew we'd need a way out with Colin." He surveyed the darkness. "He's probably out there somewhere, Joe, watching us, and is planning to put the boards in place after we've gone."

"I think you're right," Joe said. Raising his voice just a little, he added, "We've got him out. Thanks for your help! We're taking him to the hospital. We won't say anything about where we found him."

Joe actually didn't expect any kind of a reply, but just as they turned the corner of the building to head up the alley to the street where the van was parked, the man called, "I hope he's all right. Maybe I'll see you guys around sometime."

"We think he'll be all right!" Joe called to the man.

"Thanks again for your help," Frank added.

When they got to the end of the alley, Joe stopped.

"What's wrong?" Frank asked.

"I wanted to see if any cars were coming," Joe replied. "Some people might think we're carrying a dead body out of the alley."

"Yeah—I see what you mean," Frank said. "Anything coming?"

"No. It's still quiet," Joe said. "Now I'm glad this area is kind of deserted."

When they hit the street, they picked up their pace. Seeing the van gave them an adrenaline rush.

They made it to the other sidewalk, opened the back door, and put Colin on one of the seats. Joe got in beside him to hold him in place.

Frank started the engine and made a U-turn. "Next stop Bayport General Hospital emergency room!" he said.

A couple of more modern hospitals had been built in the newer parts of Bayport over the years, but the venerable old Bayport General was still at the edge of the downtown area. It usually handled most of the police calls. Frank also thought that they'd be so used to seeing patients like Colin, they might not ask too many questions.

The hospital was only five blocks from where they had been, so it didn't take them long to get there. Frank pulled the van into the emergency room parking lot, and he and Joe carried Colin to the entrance.

An orderly going in at the same time got a wheelchair, and together they took Colin into an examination room.

The hospital was either between emergencies or it had been a quiet night, because a doctor came in right away.

A nurse asked Frank if he could give her some information she needed for the hospital forms. Frank tried to be as vague as possible and made sure that the nurse knew that Colin couldn't pay for this. He told the nurse that Colin had been attacked by unknown assailants, that he was sure that Colin wasn't going to press charges, and that Colin wanted to get out of there as soon as possible.

"We can't force you to have any tests," the doctor was telling Colin when Frank finished with the nurse. "But at least let me clean the wounds and put some medicine on them."

Colin agreed to that.

Joe used the time to call the Randles and asked to talk to Nella. He told her Colin was all right, but he decided not to go into detail. "Trust me and Frank," Joe said. "We're taking care of things. You might also tell your parents that Colin is planning to spend the night with us."

Thirty minutes later, they were leaving the hospital.

"Next stop, a hot shower and a soft bed!" Frank said.

"Not me," Colin said. "I have something better in mind."

Joe looked over at Colin. He thought that some of the swelling in Colin's face had gone down, but it was still puffy in places. "What?" he asked.

"I want Melanie and her father to see what her boyfriend did to me," Colin said. "They went too far this time. I've got to fight back."

"Oh, I don't know about that, Colin. I think it might be better to sleep on it," Frank said. "We can talk to Dad and see what he'd do."

"Frank's right, Colin," Joe said. "It's too late tonight to—"

"Stop the van!" Colin shouted.

When Frank didn't let up on the accelerator, Colin said, "If you don't stop this van, I'll jump out. I mean it. I'm going to talk to the Johnsons tonight!"

Frank and Joe looked at each other. They knew Colin was serious. They also knew that they couldn't let him do this by himself.

"Call Dad," Frank finally said. "Tell him to meet us in front of the Johnson's house."

Joe used his cell phone to call their father.

Some of the Hardy boys' friends could have expected a lecture if they had called their parents around midnight, but Mr. and Mrs. Hardy trusted Frank and Joe implicitly and knew that they were probably involved in something that had to do with solving a mystery.

Joe explained to Mr. Hardy everything that had happened during the evening.

"Colin wants to confront the Johnsons. He wants them to see what Melanie's boyfriend did to him," Joe said. "We can't talk him out of it, Dad, so we need you there," he added in a whisper.

Fenton Hardy agreed to come. He told the boys he'd meet them outside the Johnsons' house in twenty minutes.

When the Hardy boys reached the Johnsons' house, the neighborhood was all dark, and there were no other vehicles on the street. Frank parked the van at the edge of the Johnsons' property, under the branches of a big tree that offered a little cover.

Fenton Hardy arrived right on schedule and parked behind the boys' van. He examined Colin and was stunned at what he saw. "Are you really sure you feel up to this?" he asked.

Colin nodded. "Yes, I want to confront them. I have to do it tonight."

The four of them walked up to the Johnsons' front door, and Fenton Hardy rang the bell.

After several minutes, a maid in a housecoat answered. She wasn't in a very good mood.

"I want to see Mr. and Mrs. Johnson and Melanie," Colin said. "Now!"

"Do you know what time it is?" the maid demanded.

"Look at me!" Colin said. "This happened because of the Johnsons. Tell them that Colin Randles wants to talk to them!"

The maid let out a big sigh and said, "Just a minute," and closed the door without asking them inside.

Ten minutes later, the front door opened. Mr. and Mrs. Johnson and Melanie were standing together, silhouetted by a light in the foyer.

"What's the meaning of this?" Mr. Johnson demanded.

"Take a good look at this young man's face,

Mr. Johnson," Fenton said. "If my sons here hadn't found him when they did he might not be alive now."

"What's this got to do with me?" Mr. Johnson said. "I don't know this young man."

Mr. Johnson's attitude was beginning to irritate Frank and Joe.

Joe nodded at Melanie. "Your daughter does, Mr. Johnson," he said.

"We were sitting behind her and her friends at the movies tonight," Frank added. "We overheard her say her boyfriend had plans for Colin Randles."

Mr. and Mrs. Johnson looked at Melanie.

"They're lying, Daddy," Melanie said. "George wouldn't do anything like that."

Mr. Johnson looked back at the Hardys. "Did you see this attack take place?" he asked them.

Joe and Frank shook their heads.

Mr. Johnson turned toward Colin. "Can you identify the person who did this to you?" he asked.

Colin shook his head. "I thought it was Frank Hardy who called me at home. When I got to the building, this guy was waiting for me right inside the alley. It was dark, but he sort of looked like Frank, too."

"We talked to a homeless man who takes shelter in the building," Frank explained. "He saw it."

"You talked to a homeless person? Oh, well, now there's a voice of authority!" Mr. Johnson said. "I think maybe you two beat Colin up yourself and for some reason you're trying to cause trouble for my daughter."

"Now just a minute, Mr. Johnson," Fenton Hardy said. "You can't accuse . . . "

"I think Melanie was kidnapped when she was two or three years old," Colin said, interrupting Mr. Hardy.

Mr. Johnson's face suddenly went purple. "Either you leave my property now, or I'm going to call the police," he shouted at them. With that, he slammed the door in their faces.

10 The Randles Leave Bayport

For a couple of minutes, the Hardys and Colin stood staring at the Johnson's front door. Finally Mr. Hardy said, "It's late, boys. We need to get home. I've got some thinking to do."

Frank, Joe, and Colin piled into the van. Colin let out a groan as he collapsed into the seat. Joe did a U-turn and got behind Mr. Hardy's car.

"I think you're going to be really sore in the morning," Joe told him.

"I'm already really sore, Joe," Colin said. "I probably need to take some aspirin when I get to your house."

"Mom and Aunt Gertrude will know what to do," Frank added. "They're used to playing doctor at our house. Joe and I have been known to get in a few scrapes of our own from time to time."

When they arrived at the Hardy house, Mrs. Hardy and Aunt Gertrude were waiting for them. It was obvious that Mr. Hardy had used his cell phone to inform them of everything that had happened over the course of the evening.

"Good heavens!" Aunt Gertrude exclaimed when she saw Colin. "You look terrible!"

"You boys need to go on to bed," Mrs. Hardy said. "Your aunt Gertrude and I will take care of Colin. He can sleep in the guest bedroom."

Neither of the boys argued. A shower and a soft bed sounded really good to both of them.

After they had their pajamas on and were in bed, though, Frank said, "I think I'm too keyed up to sleep."

"Me too," Joe said, and shook his head. "Can you believe Mr. Johnson, trying to make it seem like we had beaten up Colin and were trying to put the blame on Melanie's boyfriend?"

"I know!" Frank said. "And if you want to know the truth, I'd take the word of a homeless person any day over the word of Mr. Johnson. He's one of those men who thinks he owns the world."

"That's the impression I got, too," Joe agreed. "I guess you can't blame Melanie for acting the way she does." He yawned and leaned his head back against the pillow. In a couple of minutes, he was sound asleep.

Frank turned out the overhead light. He turned on his beside lamp and read a couple of pages in a book before he, too, decided it was time for sleep.

The next morning, even Frank and Joe weren't prepared for Colin's face. It was yellow, purple, black, and blue.

"Do you think you should stay home?" Joe asked. "You're going to scare a lot of people."

Colin tried to smile but he hurt so much that he ended up only grimacing. "Maybe I'll get some sympathy votes," he said.

"I wouldn't count on it," Frank said. "After what I saw last night, Melanie will probably have a really elaborate story concocted that a lot of people will believe."

"Well, it doesn't really matter, Frank, because I don't intend to let anyone, including the Johnsons, stop me this time," Colin said. "I know what I'm talking about, whether Melanie wants to believe me or not. She's not who she thinks she is. She was kidnapped when she was little."

Mrs. Hardy had prepared breakfast. Unfortunately, it was hard for Colin to open his mouth wide enough for food and Frank and Joe were still groggy from a late night, so most of breakfast was left untouched.

The boys grabbed their books—except for Colin,

who said that all of his were in his locker at school—and headed out to the van.

When they reached Bayport High School, a crowd had gathered at the spot where Frank usually parked. It was a friendly group, consisting of Chet, Iola, Callie, Tony, and Phil.

When they saw Colin, they all let out a gasp.

"It's all over school, Colin," Callie said. "Melanie said you attacked her boyfriend and he had to defend himself."

Joe looked at Colin. "What'd I tell you?" To their friends he said, "That's not exactly how it happened."

"Not exactly," Frank repeated. As they all walked toward the front door of the school, Frank told them the real story.

"Well, I thought Melanie's version sounded made-up," Phil said. "She seemed too interested in making sure that everyone in school heard it."

"I've never seen this boyfriend of hers," Frank said. "Do any of you know George?"

"He moved here from New York City a couple of years ago," Callie said. "Mr. Johnson brought him in to take care of the urban renewal property the bank was buying downtown."

Frank and Joe looked at each other. George would have a key to the front door of the building where they found Colin.

The school day turned out to be relatively uneventful. Most of the other kids either ignored

Colin or just gave him a passing glance. Evidently, it didn't make much difference to those who weren't Melanie's friend if Colin had attacked Melanie's boyfriend or not. George wasn't a student at Bayport High School, which meant he wasn't a part of their daily lives.

By the end of the day, when Frank and Joe met Colin at the van, the Hardys had decided that things might start getting back to normal sooner than they thought.

"You're welcome to spend another night with us," Joe said, as Frank started out of the parking lot. "We can plan our strategy and maybe even talk about developing our psychic abilities."

"No. I need to go home. My parents will probably be worried about me," Colin said. "I'm sure Nella made up some pretty good excuse—she's good at doing that—but I need to let them know everything that happened."

"Whatever you say," Frank said. "But just remember that you're always welcome."

Colin thought for a minute. "You know something—my parents probably won't be home until late, because they've been putting in long hours at Mr. Shaw's hardware store. So if you could drop me there, that would be great. I can go ahead and talk to them about this now. I just want to get it off my chest. I already feel bad about the trouble I've caused."

"We can do that," Frank said, "but you shouldn't feel bad about anything, Colin."

"You're not the one who's causing the trouble," Joe added. "You were just trying to let Melanie Johnson know what happened to her when she was a little girl."

"I'm still getting those strong feelings, guys. I got them last night when I was looking at her eyes," Colin said. "I felt them today in school when I was walking down the hall. Melanie was probably nearby. They're strong enough now that I don't even have to touch her."

They rode in silence for another ten minutes until they reached Shaw's Hardware Store. Just as they parked in front, a police car pulled up behind them. Two officers jumped out and ran into the hardware store.

"I don't feel good about this," Colin said. Wincing from pain, he jumped out of the van and ran after the police officers. Frank and Joe followed.

Inside, several kids were milling around at the rear of the store. Frank recognized them as high school friends of Melanie Johnson.

"Mom! Dad!" Colin called. "What's going on?"

Several of the kids looked up, pointed at Colin, and started laughing. He ignored them and so did the Hardy boys.

While the police officers talked to Mr. Randles, Mrs. Randles hurried over, tears in her eyes, and grabbed Colin. "Oh, Colin, what is this all about? What kind of trouble are you in?"

"I'm not in trouble, Mom," Colin assured her. "I'm not." He looked at the Hardys for help.

Frank gave her a quick, but thorough—and for the moment reassuring—explanation.

"What are these kids doing here, Mom?" Colin asked. "This is not exactly where you'd expect to find a lot of high school students."

"They've been in and out all day, and they've been robbing us blind, too," Mrs. Randles whispered. "We finally decided to call the police. We didn't do it earlier, because we didn't want any trouble." A tear rolled down her cheek. "This is a perfect job for me and my husband, and we can do it, too," she said to the Hardys. "We don't want Mr. Shaw to think we can't. But this . . ." She waved her hand toward the back of the store where Melanie's friends were standing around, giggling.

Joe could tell that Colin was seething. He wasn't going to let these punks do this to his parents. Just as Colin started for the back of the store, Joe grabbed his arm. "It's not worth it, Colin. You can't win this. The police are here now. Let them take care of it."

After a few minutes, the police officers told the teenagers to leave. They sauntered out, making sure they came by where Colin and the Hardy boys were standing.

"Your parents are in serious trouble. You don't accuse somebody of shoplifting if you can't prove it," one of the kids said to Colin. "But don't worry. Our lawyers will take care of it."

He and his friends burst into laughter.

When the last teenager was out of the store, Colin opened his mouth to say something—but his mother started crying, so he hugged her close to him and let her put her head on his shoulder.

"It's all my fault, Mom. It's all my fault," he said. "I should never have said what I did, but I thought Melanie Johnson would want to know that she had been kidnapped."

Mr. Randles had walked the police officers to the front door and was now headed back to where the Hardy boys were standing with Colin and his mother.

Mrs. Randles looked up, wiped her eyes, and said, "Are they going to do anything?"

Mr. Randles shook his head. "We didn't catch any of them in the act," he said. "So we can't prove it."

"Is that all the police said, Dad?" Colin asked.

"Well, that's all they *said*," Mr. Randles replied. He got a disgusted look on his face. "But I got the distinct impression that these were kids the police are used to letting off with a slap on the wrist."

"You're probably right," Frank said. "At school, most of them are usually hanging around Melanie Johnson."

"She evidently gets them to do her dirty work," Joe added.

"I don't remember anything like this happening before," Frank said. "Usually, the different groups at school get along very well—or at least they tolerate each other."

"That was before I arrived on the scene," Colin said, "and disrupted Melanie Johnson's nice, secure little world."

"You know, you may have something there, Colin," Frank said. "This looks like a case of over-reaction to me. I think you've touched a nerve. I think you're telling the Johnsons something they don't want to hear."

"Please don't encourage him, Frank," Mr. Randles pleaded. "We're trying to get Colin to suppress his psychic abilities and ignore the messages he receives."

"Can you do that?" Joe asked.

"If you don't follow up on things, if you just ignore them, then yes," Mrs. Randles said, "you can make yourself less psychic. Colin knows the trouble his visions cause the family."

Mr. Randles looked at his watch. "Two hours before we close. We've got work to do. Colin, could you spare some time? We need to take inventory. I want to find out exactly what those kids stole from us today."

"Sure, Dad," Colin said. He turned to Frank and

Joe. "Thanks for the ride. You guys are great. I know I have two good friends here in Bayport."

"Could you use a couple of extra workers?" Frank asked. "We'd be free labor."

"We couldn't do that," Mrs. Randles said. "You've already wasted too much of your time with us."

"It's not a waste, Mrs. Randles," Joe said. "We'd like to help."

"Well, it would go faster with two more people to help us count," Mr. Randles said.

"Then we're hired!" Joe said.

That made everyone laugh.

Mrs. Randles gave them all inventory sheets, and they set about counting the items on the list.

They had been working for about an hour when the front door opened, and Callie's father came in. He wasn't smiling, and Frank knew that the Randles were about to hear some more bad news.

"Hello, Mr. Shaw," Mr. Randles said, trying to keep his voice as steady as possible. "We're doing a little inventory. Just a minor problem."

Mr. Shaw took a deep breath. "Well, maybe not so minor," he said.

"What do you mean?" Colin asked.

Mr. Shaw looked at Colin then back at his parents.

"I got a telephone call from the bank a few minutes ago. Mr. Johnson's bank," Mr. Shaw said. "He told me that I might start having trouble with my loans, and I've made a lot of them, because of some urban renewal projects I'm involved in. Mr. Johnson gave me a lot of banker's talk, not all of which I understood—but I did understand one thing. He let me know one way I could keep from having any problems."

"What was that?" Frank asked.

"I have to fire Mr. and Mrs. Randles," Mr. Shaw said.

11 A Change of Plans

"I understand, Mr. Shaw," Mr. Randles said. "You're just doing what you have to do."

"No, he's not!" Colin shouted. "He's caving under the worst kind of pressure."

"Colin! Stop it!" Mrs. Randles said. She turned to Mr. Shaw. "We all have to do what we have to do. My husband and I understand."

The Hardy boys looked at each other, wondering if they could say something to Mr. Shaw that would make him change his mind. In the end, they decided that Mr. Johnson was a more formidable foe than they had realized, and would do anything to get even with people who didn't leave him and his family alone.

"I'm sorry," Mr. Shaw said. "I really am."

With that, he turned and left the hardware store.

Everyone stood around for several minutes, wondering what they should do first. Looking at his watch, Mr. Randles said, "It's closing time. I'll make out the night deposit, drop that by the bank—Mr. Johnson's bank—and then we'll go on home."

Later, when the Hardy boys were on their way home, Joe said, "I'm really disappointed in Callie's dad. I never expected something like this from him."

"We may not know the whole story, Joe," Frank countered. "Sometimes people get themselves in over their heads. I know Mr. Shaw has been investing a lot in the urban renewal of downtown Bayport. He may have gotten himself so much in debt that Mr. Johnson can pull any strings he wants to pull."

"That's never going to happen to me," Joe announced. "I'm going to be on top of any investments I make."

"I'm sure Mr. Shaw thought the same thing," Frank said.

When they pulled into their driveway, they saw Mr. Hardy's car.

"I'm glad Dad's home," Joe said. "We need to let him know what just happened with the Randles."

"He won't be surprised, I'm sure," Frank said. "I got the feeling last night that he had plans to check into Mr. Johnson's business operations. Dad was really angry about how the Johnsons acted last night."

Mrs. Hardy and Aunt Gertrude had just finished setting the table for dinner, so Frank and Joe washed up and joined everyone.

"I'm starved," Joe said. "This looks really good."

"Of course it does," Aunt Gertrude told him. "What did you expect?"

It was obvious to Frank that Aunt Gertrude was in one of her "moods," so the best thing was to change the subject—even if it meant giving them the disappointing news about the Randles.

Frank detailed the events that took place at Mr. Shaw's hardware store.

"I'm sure Melanie put her friends up to it," Joe said. "They were having a really good time, making the Randles' lives miserable."

"Unfortunately, making some people unhappy is often what makes other people happy," Aunt Gertrude observed. "I don't understand what's going on in the minds of people like that."

"I don't either," Mrs. Hardy agreed.

Mr. Hardy didn't comment, but he looked pensive.

"Can we do anything about it, Dad?" Frank asked. "Will the Randles have to move?"

"I'm discovering that Mr. Johnson is a more powerful man than I had realized," Mr. Hardy said. "He has quietly been buying up a lot of property in and around downtown Bayport. He is more or less dictating what's going to happen down there."

"I spoke to Colin on the phone just before dinner. He told me that the Randles are planning to move to New York City tomorrow," Joe said. "They don't see any future in Bayport."

"Unfortunately, I have to agree with them," Mr. Hardy said. "That disappoints me too. Things like this shouldn't be happening."

There wasn't much conversation after that. Everyone's thoughts seemed to be on what they could do to help the Randles, but by the end of the meal no one had offered a plan.

After dinner, Joe called Colin again. He thought maybe just talking to him would let the whole family know that the Hardys were still their friends.

Colin told Joe that Mr. Randles had already rented a trailer, and that they were packing their belongings. "We should be ready to leave by dawn. Mom and Dad don't want to stay in Bayport any longer than they have to. We'll call the school for our transfers once we get to New York."

"Is there anything Frank and I can do?" Joe asked.

Colin thought for a minute. "Well, it's going to be a tight fit, because we couldn't afford the biggest trailer—so your van would really come in handy," he said. "Since it's the weekend, maybe you and Frank could come along. It'd be nice to have some company."

"We're in," Joe said.

After he hung up, Joe told Frank that he had offered to help the Randles move.

"Good idea," Frank said. "We need to get some more information from Colin anyway."

"More information?" Joe said. "About what?"

"You don't think we're just going to let this drop, do you?" Frank said. "The more I think about Colin's visions of Melanie, the more I'm convinced that this kidnapping did take place. Don't you think that, the way Mr. Johnson is overreacting about this whole thing? I certainly do."

"You may be right, Frank," Joe said. "Some people would have just laughed it off. They might have gotten a *little* irritated, but they wouldn't do what Mr. Johnson did."

"Unless he's basically a really mean person," Frank added, "but then I think that part of his personality would have shown itself before now."

Joe nodded. "Maybe he's scared, Frank," he said. "Maybe he knows that Colin is telling the truth."

The Hardy boys had a renewed determination to solve this mystery. Mr. Johnson may have been successful in forcing the Randles to leave Bayport, but he wouldn't have the same luck with stopping the Hardys from investigating.

The next morning, Frank and Joe were up and out of the house before dawn. They left their parents a note, telling them they were using their van to help the Randles move to New York. The boys knew that if their parents needed anything, they could reach Frank and Joe by cell phone.

"We'll never forget what you boys have done for us," Mrs. Randles told Frank and Joe. "You're the people we'll remember when we think of Bayport."

"That sounds so final, Mrs. Randles," Joe said. "Don't you ever want us to visit you in New York?"

"Of course we do. Of course," Mrs. Randles hastened to add. "It's just that, well . . ."

When she trailed off, Colin said, "It's just that in all the other places we've lived, people have been glad to see us go."

"Forget that," Frank said.

The boys and Colin made short work of packing up their van with the things in Colin's room, and just as the sun came up, they headed toward New York City.

Frank and Joe used the drive to let Colin know that they weren't going to give up trying to solve the Melanie Johnson mystery.

"It must be nice to have roots," Colin said. "That's what I'd really like, to be able to call one place home for more than a couple of weeks." He looked over at Frank. "I tried, you know. I really tried. It's just when these visions come to me, when I see things that I think might help other people, well, I have to talk about them." He shook his head in disgust. "I just wish I could keep my mouth shut."

"Quit beating yourself up, Colin," Joe said. "You didn't do anything wrong."

"My parents would probably disagree with you," Colin said.

"I doubt that, if you really pressed them," Frank said. "It's just that they're frustrated, trying to figure out how to deal with being psychic and living in a world where there are a lot of people who don't believe in psychics."

Most of the rest of the trip was taken up by listening to music on the radio and talking about movies they'd like to see.

The Randles were planning to stay with friends of Colin's mother in Williamsburg, located just over the Williamsburg Bridge in the northern section of Brooklyn.

"It'll be crowded," Colin said, "but there's a subway stop nearby that'll get me to Manhattan in a matter of minutes."

Joe knew that Colin was trying to sound happy, but he wasn't doing a very good job.

When they finally arrived, Frank parked the van behind the trailer the Randles had been pulling, and they all piled out.

The friends were Joseph and Lydia Kopsky, and they were delighted to see everyone. As far as the boys could tell, the Kopskys were really excited about the Randles staying with them until they could get a place of their own.

First, Mrs. Kopsky showed Nella to her bedroom, which she would be sharing with the Kopskys' daughter, Julia, who was the same age. The bedroom was large, newly decorated, and had a pleasant view of the backyard. Frank and Joe could tell that Nella probably wouldn't miss Bayport. Mrs. Kopsky had turned her sewing room into a bedroom for Mr. and Mrs. Randles. It was small, but it also had a view of the backyard.

Then Mr. Kopsky showed Colin his bedroom, which Colin learned he was going to have to share with Mr. Kopsky's elderly uncle. He had just moved in about a week ago, because his wife had died, and he didn't want to live by himself. Nobody seemed to think Colin would be bothered by this. Nobody, that is, except Frank and Joe.

Joe suddenly had an idea—a plan. He was sure it would work, and was surprised no one had thought of it before now.

When they all went to the dining room, where Mrs. Kopsky had set out coffee and tea and a delicious-looking cake, Joe said, "We'd like for Colin to live with us in Bayport, Mr. and Mrs. Randles—at least for the rest of the school year. I mean, we'll need to make sure this is okay with our parents, but we're positive it'll be fine."

You beat me to the punch! Frank thought.

Colin gave both of the Hardys a puzzled look, but he didn't say anything.

Mr. and Mrs. Randles looked absolutely stunned.

"Oh, never! Never!" Mrs. Randles said. "I wouldn't sleep at night, for worrying about him."

"He'd be with us most of the time, Mrs. Randles," Frank said. "He could even call you every night so you wouldn't worry."

"What would your parents say?" Mr. Randles asked. "You really would need to ask them about this."

"They'd be totally fine with it, I'm sure," Joe said. "They like Colin. They'd welcome him as part of the family."

"Well, it might not be such a bad idea," Mr. Randles said. Now he was looking at the Hardy boys with an understanding he had not had initially. Frank and Joe both were sure that they saw something in his eyes that told them he knew Colin had unfinished business in Bayport. "Colin's never had a chance to have friends like the Hardys. The more I think about it, the more I think we should let him do it."

"Well, I need to think about this," Mrs. Randles said.

"While you're thinking, we can have some coffee and cake," Mrs. Kopsky said. "That always seems to make everyone feel better."

Joe didn't normally like coffee, but he had to admit that Mrs. Kopsky's coffee tasted really great with the cake she had baked.

When everyone was finished, Mrs. Randles looked at Colin. "Nobody seems to have asked you how you feel about this, Colin," she said. "So now I'm asking you."

"I want to go," Colin said simply. "I'll miss you, but I think it's the best thing."

Mrs. Randles nodded. "You've always had a good head on your shoulders, Colin," she said. "I'm sure you'll continue to use it well."

"Then it's settled," Mr. Randles said.

Frank and Joe got into the van, while Colin said his good-byes. He thanked the Kopskys for their thoughtfulness, hugged Nella and his parents, and then got into the van.

"When did you first get this idea, Joe?" Colin asked as they headed down the street toward the Williamsburg Bridge.

"I'm not sure. I think it was when Mr. Shaw fired your mom and dad," Joe replied. "I knew we couldn't let Mr. Johnson get away with that."

Colin grinned. "Are you sure your parents won't mind? Were you just saying that for my parents' benefit?"

"Mom and Aunt Gertrude are on your side, Colin. They were really upset about what happened," Frank said. "And Dad, well, I know Dad is really angry about what Mr. Johnson did. He'll be glad you're back."

Joe grinned. "I can hardly wait until Monday

morning," he said. "When Colin shows up at school, there are going to be some really surprised people."

Colin nodded. "I don't need to worry about my parents now. Nobody can run them out of Bayport," Colin said. "And I've got some good friends. I don't have to suppress my psychic visions. I can concentrate and make them stronger.

"I'm going to find out why Melanie Johnson was kidnapped."

12 The Meeting with Melanie

Frank and Joe were right about one thing. A lot of the kids at Bayport High School were surprised to see Colin Randles walking down the hall, going to his first class. But the person they thought would be the most surprised, Melanie Johnson, acted as though there was nothing unusual about it.

"I don't trust her one bit," Joe whispered to Frank. "She's got something planned, I'm sure."

"If she doesn't, then it's probably safe to say that some of her friends do," Frank agreed. "We need to make sure one of us is with Colin at all times."

"Agreed," Joe said.

Even though Frank and Joe didn't have all the same classes that Colin did, they arranged for one of them to be outside Colin's classroom door at the

117

end of every class. This kept them running through the halls most of the day, but they succeeded.

By the time school was out, not only had nothing happened, but the people Frank and Joe thought might cause Colin trouble—like Mr. Brooks and some of Melanie's friends—seemed to be ignoring him. This seemed weird.

Just as they were heading to the van to go home, Joe's cell phone rang.

He answered it, then stopped, and motioned for Frank and Colin to stop, too.

"Well, as a matter of fact, Melanie," Joe said a little louder than he needed to, "Colin is right here. Do you want to talk to him?"

Colin had a puzzled look on his face. This was obviously something that none of them had expected.

He took the telephone from Joe. "This is Colin, Melanie," he said nonchalantly. "What's up?"

Colin listened for about ten minutes. Joe and Frank tried to read his face but it remained passive. "Okay. We'll be there." Colin punched the "end" button and handed the cell phone back to Joe.

"Where are we supposed to be?" Frank asked.

"Melanie wants us to come to her house tonight, at seven thirty," Colin replied. "Her parents will be at a banquet. She said she has something very important to tell us."

"You actually told her we'd be there?" Joe asked

incredulously. "Don't you think she might be setting a trap for us?"

"I don't think so," Colin said. "I heard something in her voice."

"Well, this could work out after all," Frank said. "I had been wondering how to get this investigation started."

"I still don't like it," Joe said. "I would have suggested a neutral meeting sight."

"We do need to work out some sort of a strategy," Frank said. "We can't just walk into her house tonight unprepared."

"Okay. I can understand that," Colin said. "I'm not sure it's really necessary, but I won't argue."

They got into the van and headed toward the Hardys' house. Their confrontation with Melanie was going to take place sooner than any of them had imagined.

At seven fifteen, Frank drove by the front of the Johnsons' house a couple of times, to see if any cars were parked in front. There weren't, but he decided that it would be smart to park the van one street over.

"Just in case," he said. "I think a little caution here is important."

Joe agreed.

Colin seemed lost in his thoughts.

"I say we scope out the place first," Frank said, "just to make sure it's not a trap."

119

The three of them got out of the van and started walking down the sidewalk. They had all worn dark clothing, so they wouldn't be any more visible than necessary.

At the corner, they turned left onto a side street that would take them to the Johnsons' house. They had planned to go in through a gate that led to the backyard and check out what was going on from there, but before they reached the gate, Joe stopped.

"That spotlight bothers me. If we use the gate someone might see us," he said. "We've been spending a lot of time developing our track and field skills; why not just vault over this fence instead? It's darker back here."

"Good thinking," Frank said.

Joe went first, taking a running jump at the fence. As he jumped up, he grabbed the top of the fence, and vaulted over.

Colin took one look at what Joe had done and said to Frank, "I think maybe you'd better give me a handhold. I think I can take care of myself after that."

Frank clasped his hands together for a hold for Colin's left foot and gave a heave, allowing Colin to catch the top of the fence and vault over.

Frank took a running jump and in one bounce was up and over the fence, landing soundlessly right in front of Joe and Colin.

"You should rethink throwing the javelin," Joe

whispered. "You've got a brighter future in the hurdles."

Frank grinned at him. "Well, I'd hate to take away all of the glory from you," he said.

"Oh, don't worry about that," Joe said, and grinned back. "You'd probably only get second place."

Frank gave him a brotherly shove. "Yeah, right! In your dreams!"

"It sure is quiet," Colin said.

Frank and Joe looked around, letting their eyes adjust to the darkness of the Johnsons' backyard.

"Maybe too quiet," Joe said. He looked at Frank. "What do you think?"

Frank shrugged. "I think we should be prepared for anything."

From where they were standing, they could see only one light on inside the house. It was in an upstairs room.

"That's probably Melanie's," Frank observed.

"I have an idea," Joe said. He took out his cell phone, punched in a number, and put the receiver to his ear. After a couple of seconds he said, "Melanie? This is Joe Hardy. Colin wanted us to come with him tonight. Okay? Uh, huh. Uh, huh. Uh, huh. That sounds good. Well, we should be there in about five minutes. See you." Joe pushed "end" on the phone and said, "She told me to just ring the front doorbell when we got here."

"How did she sound?" Colin asked.

"Tired," Joe said. "And she didn't sound like she had a bunch of people in her room waiting to play a trick on us, either."

"Well, let's wait a couple of minutes, just to see if more lights go on in the house and people start coming out of the woodwork," Frank said.

After five minutes, when nothing in the house seemed to have changed, the three of them headed toward the side gate that would take them to the front of the Johnsons' house.

Colin rang the doorbell. In a couple of seconds, an interior downstairs light came on, and right after that the front door opened.

The Hardys were still prepared for anything that might happen, but there was nobody standing behind Melanie—and from their vantage point, they couldn't see anyone else in the interior of the house.

"I'm glad you came," Melanie said. She stood aside so they could enter.

When the boys were inside, Melanie closed and locked the door. "We can go into the library," she said.

Melanie turned and led them toward the back part of the enormous house.

When they got there, Melanie shut the door and told them to have a seat. "I thought you might like some soft drinks," she said. "Just help yourself."

Joe couldn't believe how dry his mouth was, so he chose his favorite soda.

Frank and Colin didn't want anything.

"Why did you ask me here?" Colin asked. "I hope you're not planning to sic your boyfriend on me again."

"No, Colin. And I'm so sorry that I lied to you," Melanie said. "You'd be perfectly within your rights if you never believed me again."

"Why did you do it, Melanie?" Joe asked.

"I was scared. It just got out of hand, and I didn't know what to do about it after it happened."

Frank was eyeing her carefully, trying to see if she was faking, but so far she seemed very sincere.

"I wanted to tell you something I've never told anybody before," Melanie said. She took a deep breath. "Sometimes I see those same things that you see about my childhood."

Colin stared at her. *"You're psychic?"*

"Oh, no, nothing like that," Melanie assured him. "It's just that sometimes I remember . . . *things.*"

"What kinds of things?" Colin asked.

"The kinds of things you said happened to me," Melanie said. Her eyes were filling with tears. "I remember somebody taking me from my mother. I know this is silly, because my mother and my father live with me in this house, but . . . it just seems so real at times."

For an instant, the three of them could only stare at Melanie in disbelief.

"Why are you telling Colin this now, Melanie?"

Joe said. "Why did you let all of these terrible things happen to him and his family?"

"Well, why do you think, Joe?" Melanie demanded angrily. "I told you I was scared. I just thought it was some crazy dream I was remembering, and then he . . . Colin comes along and tells me the same thing."

Frank was trying to let go of some of the anger he felt toward Melanie. "Well, I guess if we'd been in your situation, we'd have felt the same way," he said.

"Still . . . ," Joe said. He was having a harder time letting it all go. He couldn't get the image of Colin's battered face out of his mind.

"I knew you were telling the truth, Colin. I just knew you were," Melanie said. "But I didn't know what to do, so I told my boyfriend about it, and he said he'd take care of it for me. I thought he was just going to talk to you. I didn't know he would . . ."

"Well, he did," Joe said. "He really—"

Colin raised his hand, signaling Joe not to continue. "Will you tell me everything?" he said to Melanie. "Don't leave anything out."

What Melanie told Colin was basically what Colin had already told the Hardy boys. Late one night, when Melanie was two years old, she remembered a man coming into her room, picking her up, and starting to leave the house. She was sure she knew the man, but in her dreams, she had never seen his face. Melanie remembered that she had started to cry, because she didn't have her little stuffed lamb with her. She always slept with the lamb. She told the man that she wanted to take the lamb with her. He promised to go back and get it for her if she would stop crying. She did.

"That's where it all goes blank," Melanie said.

"Do you still have the lamb?" Colin asked.

Melanie nodded, a little embarrassed, Frank could tell. "I still sleep with it," she said.

Joe looked at Frank and rolled his eyes.

"I need it," Colin said. "I think I might be able to find out more about what happened to you through psychometry."

"What's that?" Melanie asked.

Colin explained how sometimes the stress a person is feeling is transferred to an object, such as the stuffed lamb, and that psychics can often pick up the stress and see what was happening at the time of the crime.

That's exactly what Dad told us, Joe thought.

"It's in my room. I'll get it for you," Melanie said, walking out.

"I wonder what made her change her mind," Joe said.

Frank shrugged. "I have no idea." He turned to Colin. "Do you?"

"I think—," Colin started to say.

But outside the library, they suddenly heard voices. The three of them looked at each other.

"That sounds like Mr. Johnson!" Joe whispered. "It's a trap after all."

The three of them ran to the library door, flattening themselves against the wall, ready to sprint out if Mr. Johnson came inside.

The voices were getting more distinct.

"I thought you said that Smedley wouldn't be there!" Mr. Johnson was yelling at someone. "There's no way I'm going to sit and listen to him for an hour."

"What's come over you, Robert?" It was Mrs. Johnson's voice. "These last few weeks, you've turned into somebody I don't recognize."

"You know what's come over me, Margaret," Mr. Johnson said. "Don't pretend that you don't."

The Hardy boys and Colin looked at each other. What were the Johnsons talking about?" they wondered.

"Daddy!"

"What are you doing with that lamb, Melanie?" Mr. Johnson demanded.

"Oops—I didn't realize I still had it in my hand," Melanie said. "I was upstairs reading. I came down to get something to eat. I—"

"You're lying! What's the light doing on in the library?" Mr. Johnson demanded. "I was in there before we left for the banquet, and I remember turning it off."

"I'm not lying, Daddy! Why are you being so

mean to me lately?" Melanie said. "I went to the library to get something to read."

Frank could hear feet running toward the library. He was sure it was Mr. Johnson. The man was acting totally paranoid.

The Hardy boys looked around. There was no other way out. If Mr. Johnson found the three of them there, there's no telling what he'd do to them.

Just then, Mr. Johnson burst into the library. He had a gun in his hands.

13 Disappearance

Without thinking, Colin rushed at Mr. Johnson, head down, and rammed him in the mid-section, causing Melanie's father to double over with an *oompf* sound as the air went out of him. He dropped the gun right before he hit the floor, causing it to discharge into the room—barely missing Joe.

Mrs. Johnson, who had been walking behind her husband, screamed and rushed into the library.

The Hardy boys and Colin ran out of the library and headed for the front door, but Melanie, who was still standing at the bottom of the stairs, whispered, "No! No! This way!"

The boys changed direction and followed Melanie up the stairs.

"George drove my parents to the banquet. He's still parked in front of the house," Melanie whispered. "I'll show you how to get out through the backyard."

Frank wondered why George hadn't rushed into the house when the gun discharged.

As if in answer to his unspoken question, Melanie said, "He listens to loud music when he's in the car by himself. He wouldn't have heard the gun."

"Why are you dating this guy, Melanie?" Joe asked.

"It was my father's idea, and I've always done what he told me to do," Melanie said. "But that's over. So is my relationship with George."

When they reached the second floor, they followed Melanie to a second floor sitting room that overlooked the backyard.

"There are fire stairs off this room," Melanie whispered. "Just follow the white flagstone path. It twists and turns, but it'll lead you to a gate in the alley."

"Thanks, Melanie," Colin said. "Are you going to be all right?"

"Don't worry about me! You have to hurry," Melanie said. "I'll call you, Colin. Now more than ever, we need to talk."

With that, the Hardy boys and Colin hurried down the back steps and into the moonlight of the backyard. Just as Melanie had said, the flagstone path twisted and turned but eventually led them to the alley. The gate obviously wasn't used very much, because it required both Joe and Frank to pry it open.

"That's good," Colin observed. "Maybe no one will think it's how we got out."

"This way!" Frank said as he started down the alley toward the street where they had parked the van.

Just before they left the alley, they stopped to make sure that George wasn't waiting for them. He wasn't.

They hopped into the van and within minutes, Frank had them out of the neighborhood and on a street that would take them to the Hardys' house.

"I'm worried about Melanie," Colin said. "I have a bad feeling about all of this."

Frank and Joe agreed.

"I'll talk to her tomorrow at school and make sure she's all right," Colin said. "Maybe we'll even have time to continue what we started talking about tonight."

When the Hardy boys and Colin arrived at school the next morning, Callie and Iola met them at the front door with the news that Melanie Johnson had withdrawn from school.

"Are you serious?" Joe said.

Callie nodded. "We were in the office this morning and overheard Mr. Brooks talking to Mrs. Johnson," she said.

"But he's not to let anyone know about it," Iola added. "He's just supposed to tell her teachers that she's sick."

"That's strange," Frank said. "Are you sure you didn't misunderstand Mr. Brooks?"

Callie shook her head. "I'm positive," she insisted.

All morning, the Hardy boys and Colin questioned people about why Melanie wasn't in school. The only answer they got was that she was sick but would probably be back in a few days.

Finally, at lunch, Callie said, "I can call the Johnsons' house, say that I know Melanie is sick, but that I'm putting together a committee to decide the theme of the next school dance, and that I want Melanie to be on it, but that I have to have her answer today."

Everyone thought that was a great idea.

Joe lent Callie his cell phone. They all crowded around, so they could hear every word of whatever conversation transpired.

Unfortunately, there wasn't much to hear.

Mrs. Johnson answered the telephone and, when Callie asked her about the committee, snapped that Melanie wouldn't be interested, because she might be in the hospital for a long time.

"Maybe she really is sick," Iola said. "Maybe we did misunderstand Mr. Brooks."

"Melanie was perfectly healthy last night," Colin said. "I don't think she's sick at all."

131

"After school, we'll call all of the hospitals in the Bayport area," Frank said. "When we find out which one she's in, we'll go visit her."

When the Hardy boys and Colin got home that afternoon, the first thing they did was get out the Bayport telephone directory and make a list of all of the hospitals in the area—public and private.

Joe started calling. "She's not in one of the public hospitals," he announced when he hung up from the last call.

"We should have known that would be a waste of time," Frank said. "Mr. Johnson wouldn't use one of the public hospitals."

But Joe didn't have any more luck with the private hospitals.

"If she's not in a Bayport hospital, then she could be anywhere," Frank said. "We can't start calling all of the hospitals on the East Coast."

"Wait a minute. Wait a minute," Colin said. "Let me see the telephone directory."

Joe handed it to him. "I don't think I missed any of the hospitals, Colin," he said. "Bayport's not so big that there's a really long list."

Colin had opened the yellow pages to the "P's" and was using his finger to scan the entries. "The problem is that we've been calling 'normal' hospitals," he said, "but if I know Mr. Johnson, that's not what he had in mind. Here's what I was looking for.

Bayport Reflections—a private psychiatric hospital."

"You think he had her committed!" Frank exclaimed.

"It wouldn't be the first time a parent did that to a child who wasn't behaving the way the parent wanted the child to behave," Colin said. "I say we call and find out."

"Those places won't give out any information over the phone," Joe said.

"Watch this," Colin said. He picked up the telephone, looked at the number in the directory, and dialed. Within a few seconds, he was using a feminine voice, punctuated with sobs, to tell the person on the other end that she had lain down for a nap before dinner, had dozed off, and had had a horrible nightmare about her darling daughter, Melanie Johnson, and that she was just calling to make sure Melanie was all right. Could this person please just check on her, so her mother could rest in peace for the rest of the evening?

Frank and Joe looked at each other and shook their heads. It was a performance worthy of an Oscar.

Colin was silent for several minutes, then, using the same voice—but this time a little less hysterical—thanked the person profusely and said he would make sure that the manager of the hospital heard about how kind she had been.

When Colin hung up the phone, he said, "She's there. In fact, I even know what room she's in, because when the nurse got back, she apologized for how long it took, because, she said, Melanie was in the Newman wing, Room 342."

"I think we just acquired a partner, Frank," Joe said.

Colin raised an eyebrow. "A partner?"

"Well, we've talked for years about starting a detective agency when we get out of school," Frank said. "I'm sure we'll need another partner."

"Right now, that doesn't sound half bad," Colin said. "Maybe by the time we're out of school, psychic detectives won't be thought of as freaks."

"Okay. We need to plan," Frank said. "What do we do with this news?"

"Well, we definitely don't sit on it," Colin said. "They may be giving Melanie medicine that will affect her ability to remember the details of the kidnapping."

"Of course!" Joe said. "Mr. Johnson definitely doesn't want Melanie thinking about this."

"If he really cared for her, he'd want to know why she, too, thinks she was kidnapped when she was about two," Colin said.

The Hardy boys and Colin knew they'd have to wait until dark before they could pursue any plan to talk to Melanie at Bayport Reflections. They killed some time catching up on their homework, but it was hard for them to concentrate.

Mr. Hardy was back in New York on another case

and Aunt Gertrude had a headache, so Mrs. Hardy said it was all right if the boys wanted to watch television in the den while they ate their dinner. They decided it might be fun to watch a rerun of a show that had been popular a few years back. It made them laugh and helped pass the time until they decided that it was time to go to Bayport Reflections to talk to Melanie.

At a few minutes before seven, Frank said, "I bet a new shift starts at the hospital at seven. If it's like most places, people stand around and talk for a few minutes before they start their shifts. I think we should get going."

Frank told Mrs. Hardy that they were going out but that they probably wouldn't be back late.

Bayport Reflections was only four miles from where the Hardys lived. It was surrounded by a dense growth of trees, making it almost invisible from the road. Frank turned in at the main drive and parked at the edge of the visitors' parking lot, in a part of the lot that wasn't well lit.

"We need to find the Newman wing first," Colin said. "Room 342."

"I'm sure they have security cameras. Someone could be watching us night now," Joe said. "I say we skirt the edge of the parking lot."

"Good idea, Joe," Frank said. "The security cameras are usually trained on the cars, so whoever is watching can make sure nobody breaks into them."

Once they reached the building, Joe said, "Let's find a service entrance. They're usually not guarded very well, because the employees are so used to seeing people in and out all the time."

The service entrance was on the southwest side, at the end of a drive. The boys followed the road inside and stopped.

"What now?" Colin asked.

"We wait," Joe said.

After a few minutes, a custodian opened the service entrance, propped open the door, disappeared inside, and then came out a few minutes later, smoking a cigarette. He started walking around the building, away from where the boys were standing.

"Where's he going?" Colin asked.

"He's going to circle the building while he smokes a cigarette," Joe replied. "It suddenly occurred to me that most hospitals don't allow employees to smoke inside the buildings anymore, so you see a lot of the employees milling around outside. This guy probably doesn't have a key to the door, so he props it open while he takes his break."

The three of them ran to the open service door and made their way through a storage area.

"Now to find the Newman wing," Joe said.

"I think we're in it," Frank said. "This part of the building doesn't look all that old."

They came to a couple of swinging doors with round windows that allowed them to look into the next section of the building. There didn't seem to be anybody around. Joe noticed a door at the end of the hallway that said EXIT.

"There should be some stairs on the other side of that door," he said. "I say we check it out."

"Well, we certainly can't wait here," Frank said. "That's as good a choice as any."

Slowly, Frank opened the swinging doors, stuck his head through, and looked in both directions. To his right, there was nothing, but to his left, farther down the hall, a couple of men dressed in white shirts and pants were wheeling a gurney—but they were wheeling it in the opposite direction of the boys.

"Looks clear," Frank whispered.

He held the door open, allowing Joe and Colin to slip through and race for the exit at the end of the hall. He was right behind them.

They made it through the door, stopped to listen for anything that might indicate someone had seen them, and then, when they didn't hear anything, started up the stairs.

"If anybody finds us, we'll just tell them that we're friends of Melanie's," Joe whispered, "and that we're slipping in to see her, because her father doesn't like us."

Frank grinned.

They made it to the second floor and started up to the third. When they reached the door to the main corridor, Frank stuck his head through, then pulled it back quickly.

"This place is pretty busy," he said.

They waited a few more minutes, then Frank stuck his head through the door again.

"It's not as busy now," he said, when he pulled his head back in. "I think we can make it. At least Melanie's room is in the opposite direction and away from the brighter lights of the nurses' station."

Quietly, the three of them slipped into the hallway and started toward Room 342.

When they reached it, they found the door partially open. Frank could see Melanie inside. She was asleep.

"Well, here goes," Frank said.

Together, the three of them entered Melanie's room and walked over to her bed.

Suddenly, the overhead lights went on, momentarily blinding the Hardy boys and Colin.

They wheeled around.

There, blocking the door, was Mr. Johnson.

"Which one of you talked to the nurse on the phone?"

"I did," Colin said.

Mr. Johnson smiled. "I might have known. She got suspicious and called me," he said. "She told me about the dream 'my wife' had." He laughed.

"This time you won't get away," he added. "I'm going to make sure of that."

14 Confession Time

Colin stepped toward Mr. Johnson.

"I'm ready for you this time, Colin," Mr. Johnson said. "If you try anything, I'll break your neck."

"What are you afraid of, Mr. Johnson?" Colin said. He was still moving toward Mr. Johnson, ignoring his threat. "What are you afraid of?"

"How dare you talk to me that way, you scum!" Mr. Johnson shouted at Colin. He almost spit out the words. "I'm not afraid of anything!"

"Oh, I think you are! I think you're very afraid," Colin continued. "I think you've got something to hide. I think you're—"

Before Colin could finish his sentence, Mr. Johnson lunged at him and grabbed Colin around the throat.

"Daddy!" Melanie screamed. "Stop it!"

Frank and Joe immediately grabbed Mr. Johnson's arms, trying to twist his hands away from Colin's neck. They were astonished at how strong the man was.

Colin's face was beginning to turn purple.

"You can't do this to my family! I won't let you destroy us!" Mr. Johnson was shouting at Colin.

Frank and Joe were surprised to see tears trickling down Mr. Johnson's face.

Just then, Mrs. Johnson, accompanied by an orderly and a nurse, rushed into the room.

The orderly grabbed Mr. Johnson around the waist and started squeezing him. That did the trick. Mr. Johnson turned loose of Colin's neck.

Joe and Frank pulled Colin back over toward the wall, far away from Mr. Johnson's reach, in case he decided to attack Colin again. They checked Colin out to make sure he was all right.

Mr. Johnson had sunk to the floor and was on his knees, sobbing.

The Hardy boys and Colin were stunned by what they were now seeing from a man who just moments before had been one of the biggest bullies in Bayport.

Mrs. Johnson was kneeling on the floor beside her husband. "It's over, Robert! It's over," she was saying to him softly. "I never thought it would work. We made a terrible mistake, and we'll have to pay for it."

The Hardy boys and Colin looked at each other. What was Mrs. Johnson talking about?

Mrs. Johnson cradled Mr. Johnson's head on her shoulder and started patting the back of his head. "It's over, Robert. It's over," she repeated, this time more softly.

"What are you talking about, Mrs. Johnson?" Frank said. "What's over?"

Mrs. Johnson looked up him, blinked, then looked back down at her husband. "I think you need to call your lawyer, Robert," she said.

After a few moments, Mr. Johnson nodded. The orderly helped him up off the floor. He turned to Melanie, who now was standing beside her bed, pale and shaking. "I'm sorry, baby. I did what I thought was right," he said, tears streaming down his face. To Colin and the Hardy boys, he said, "Melanie is free to go. I'd appreciate it if you'd take her wherever she wants to stay tonight. If it's a hotel, she's got her credit cards. If she wants to stay at a friend's house, then I'll certainly understand that. But if she wants to come home, it's still her home and always will be. Tomorrow, I'd like to see all of you at my lawyer's office. Melanie knows the address."

With that, he and Mrs. Johnson followed the orderly and the nurse out of the room.

Melanie stared at them as they left, her eyes now almost swollen from crying. Colin walked over to her and put his arm around her.

"This is not exactly how I thought this night would end," Joe whispered to Frank.

"Me either," Frank said. "I'd say we're in for a big surprise tomorrow, except I have a pretty good idea of what to expect."

Joe nodded.

It took several minutes for Melanie to regain her composure. When she finally did, she told the Hardy boys that she wanted to stay over at her friend Bonnie Blake's. She stayed over there so often that she kept several changes of clothes and toiletries there.

Colin and the Hardy boys waited outside the room while Melanie dressed and repacked her small suitcase. They used the same stairs the boys had come up to leave the hospital. No one said anything to them on their way out.

Once in the van, Colin said, "Are you sure you're going to be all right, Melanie?"

Melanie nodded. "Yes. I'm just tired."

The rest of the trip was made in silence. When they got to Bonnie's house, Melanie said, "You've given me back part of my life, Colin, but I'll still need your help getting *all* of it back."

"I'll be there for you, Melanie," Colin said.

Melanie didn't want anyone to walk her to the door, but the boys waited until she was inside Bonnie's house before they headed home.

The next morning, the Hardys and Colin drove to the offices of Stanley, Stanley, and Stanley, high-powered corporate lawyers whose modern building was in a new development north of downtown Bayport.

Frank parked the van, and he, Joe, and Colin headed into the building, which was five stories of tinted glass. A receptionist greeted them by name with a gleaming smile that would have sold a lot of toothpaste.

"I'll take you to the conference room," she said. "Everyone else is already there."

"Are we late?" Joe asked, looking at this watch. "I thought Mr. Johnson said—"

"No, no, you're not late," the receptionist said, interrupting him. "Everyone else is early."

The Hardy boys looked at each other. It was obvious that the Johnsons wanted to get this taken care of as soon as possible.

The elevator took them silently to the top floor. When the doors opened, they were turned over to another receptionist whose job it was to take them to the conference room.

"Things have certainly changed within the last twenty-four hours, haven't they?" Joe whispered to Colin. "I think I prefer being on Mr. Johnson's A-list instead of his Z-list."

Colin nodded, but Joe could tell that he was starting to get really tense.

Joe patted him on the shoulder. "It's going to be

all right, Colin. We're no longer the enemy."

When the second receptionist opened the door, they weren't greeted by their idea of a typical conference room, with a long table surrounded by chairs. This conference room looked more like an exquisitely decorated living room, with soft couches and chairs strategically but unobtrusively placed where everyone could see everyone else. Coffee tables were stocked with plates of muffins and rolls, bottles of water, and different kinds of juices.

Mr. Johnson walked up to the Hardys and offered his hand. "Good morning," he said.

Frank thought it was more businesslike than friendly, but it certainly wasn't unfriendly.

Joe noticed that Melanie was sitting with Bonnie on a sofa close to the front of the room. She waved at them, but she didn't get up. She still had a strained look on her face. Joe doubted that she had gotten much sleep the night before.

Frank looked around the room. Mr. and Mrs. Johnson were there, of course, as well as Melanie and Bonnie. There were several people in the room Frank didn't recognize. He assumed they were members of the law firm.

"Would everyone please be seated?" Mr. Johnson said.

Almost as if it had been choreographed, the entire gathering was in place within a few seconds.

Joe helped himself to a little muffin and a glass of

orange juice. Frank took a glass of apple juice but nothing else. Colin ignored the food, not taking his eyes off of Melanie. She glanced in his direction from time to time, always with a smile on her face.

"I am here to make a confession. I could have certainly done this at home, but I wanted to make sure nothing I said could be misinterpreted or misunderstood," Mr. Johnson said. "What I am about to say will be a legal deposition." He looked at Melanie, cleared his throat, and continued. "I kidnapped my daughter when she was two years old."

There was an audible gasp from Melanie.

The Hardys had been prepared to hear those words, but they still somehow sounded totally out of character for Mr. Johnson.

Frank noticed that Melanie had now bowed her head and was crying. Bonnie had put her arm around Melanie's shoulders.

What followed was an incredible admission.

Mr. Johnson had divorced Melanie's mother before Melanie was born, because he found out his wife had kept some significant secrets. She had been in prison for writing hot checks. The divorce took place before Mr. Johnson knew that Melanie's mother was pregnant. When Mr. Johnson found out that he was going to be a father, he tried to get his former wife to let him have the baby to raise. She refused. After Melanie was born, Mr. Johnson tried to get partial custody of her, but again, his former wife refused. When Mr. Johnson discovered that Melanie's mother was not only writing hot checks again, but had remarried someone he considered a very unsavory character, he couldn't stand the thought of his beautiful child living with them. He legally changed his name; then he went to his ex-wife's home one night, and when she and her new husband were asleep, Mr. Johnson took Melanie.

He then moved to New York City with his young daughter, where he met the current Mrs. Johnson. He confessed to her what he had done and together, they decided to get married, move to Bayport, and start a new life. They knew that everyone would just assume that Mrs. Johnson was Melanie's mother. Mr. Johnson had completely lost touch with Melanie's real mom.

When Mr. Johnson finished, there was total silence in the room—until Melanie walked up to him and kissed him on the cheek.

"You did what you thought you had to do, Daddy," Melanie said. "I love you. I'll always love you."

Then everyone in the room watched as Melanie joined Colin and the Hardy boys. "Can you help me find my real mother?" she asked. "I think I'd like to talk to her."

"I think I can, Melanie," Colin said. "I honestly think I can."

15 Hostage!

The next morning at breakfast, Colin picked up the copy of the *Bayport Times* off the dining room table. He quickly scanned it, and said, "I thought there'd be something in the newspaper this morning about Mr. Johnson's confession."

"Nope," Joe said. He took a bite of scrambled eggs. "I'm sure his lawyers have seen to it that it's kept under wraps."

"So nobody knows about it?" Colin said.

"Oh, I'm sure they do," Frank said. "I'm sure it's all over Bayport—but it's just not going to be on the national news."

"Or even the local news," Joe added.

Colin shook his head. "It's amazing what money can buy."

"I'm sure Mr. Johnson doesn't see anything unusual about it," Frank said. "He confessed, so now he's the good guy."

"I talked to Melanie this morning. She hasn't changed her mind," Colin said. "She still wants me to help her find her mother. I told her we'd come over this morning."

At ten thirty, the Hardys and Colin got in the van and headed over to Melanie's house.

Joe laughed. "You know, doing this is making me a little nervous. I keep thinking that as soon as we get there, Mr. Johnson is going to come charging out of the house holding a gun."

"I think those days are over," Frank said, "but I'm not expecting a really warm welcome."

"Dad talked to some of his contacts in the Bayport Police Department about the case. He told me about it this morning before he left for New York," Joe said. "They're uncertain as to how they should proceed—or even if they *should* proceed."

"What Mr. Johnson did was illegal," Colin said. "He didn't have custody of Melanie."

"I know," Joe said, "but from what the Bayport Police learned, Melanie's mother didn't even file a missing persons report. She just left town. There's no telling where she is."

"She probably knew what had happened—that Mr. Johnson had kidnapped Melanie," Frank surmised. "She probably knew that she'd have a hard time getting her back."

"I have a feeling she might have wanted the kidnapping to happen," Joe said. "Maybe she had decided that Melanie shouldn't be around her new husband. Or maybe she just didn't care."

"That's what I'm afraid of," Colin said.

"What do you mean?" Frank asked.

"Melanie wants to find her mother. Sometimes these missing relatives don't exactly want to be reunited," Colin explained. "Many times it's better if you just forget it."

"You know Melanie's not going to be able to do that, Colin," Joe said. "She's clearly looking for some closure. I think I'd feel the same way."

"I know, I know," Colin said. "I just wanted to let you in on what might happen."

Frank turned onto Melanie's street, drove a couple of blocks, parked in front of her house, and the three of them climbed out of the van.

Melanie was at the door, waiting for them. So were Mr. and Mrs. Johnson.

Mr. Johnson shook hands with all three of the boys. "As you know, Melanie wants to locate her real mother. I'm sure you can understand why, though, we don't want to put an ad in the newspaper," he said. "She told me she thought you could do it because you're . . ."

"Psychic?" Colin offered.

Mr. Johnson nodded. "I don't claim to understand any of this, but Melanie trusts you, so I trust you, too."

"This really is the best way, Mr. Johnson, because often the person you're searching for turns out to be someone you don't really want to know at all," Colin said. "If you contact the police department, or even if you use private detectives, too many people hear about it. I can tell Melanie things that only she and I will know about," Colin said. "If you do a psychic search, you just have more control over the situation."

"Yes, that's it. That's it exactly," Mr. Johnson said. "I'm glad you understand what I mean."

"If you need anything, just ask for it," Mrs. Johnson said.

"I need the mother's name," Colin said.

"Mary," Mr. Johnson said. "Her maiden name was Davis, and I think the man she married was named Sullivan, but I'm not sure."

"I can work with that," Colin said.

Melanie started toward the library, but Colin stopped her. "I think we'd have more luck in your room, Melanie," he said. He turned to Mr. and Mrs. Johnson. "Do you mind? That's where most of Melanie's energy would be, and that's very important."

"If Melanie doesn't mind, then it's certainly all right with us," Mr. Johnson said.

"I don't mind. It's kind of a mess, though," Melanie said, and she blushed. "I just thought we'd all be more comfortable somewhere else."

"We're not going to take photos for a magazine," Joe said. He grinned at her. "And we promise not to give away your secret."

"Don't mind him, Melanie," Frank said, as they headed up the stairs to the second floor. "You should see the messes Joe makes sometimes. It's not pretty, I can tell you."

When they got to Melanie's room, the Hardy boys were surprised. They gave each other a look that said, if Melanie thinks this is a mess, she'd think our room was a disaster area.

There was a sitting area in one corner of the large room, where four plush chairs surrounded a table.

"When I have sleepovers, this is where we eat or play cards or just sit and talk," Melanie said.

"This is perfect," Colin told her. "What I need from you now is your stuffed lamb."

The Hardy boys could see the little stuffed lamb lying on one of Melanie's pillows.

She really does *sleep with it,* Frank thought.

Melanie went over to her bed and grabbed the lamb. "You said you were going to use . . . *psy* . . . I don't remember the word."

"*Psychometry,*" Colin said. "A person's body gives off electromagnetic or biomagnetic energy,

151

and this energy leaves an impression on some material object."

"How long does it stay?" Melanie asked. "I've had this lamb for a long time. It's not in very good shape."

"It's fine," Colin told her. "These impressions remain forever."

"That's hard to believe," Joe said.

Colin gave him a puzzled look.

"Oh, no, what I meant is that it's so incredible, that it's just hard to believe that something like that sort of 'impressioning' exists," Joe tried to explain, "but I believe it. I know I'm not making any sense."

"That's what *I* believe!" Frank said.

Everyone laughed, and that broke some of the tension that had begun to develop.

"I know what you mean," Colin said. "I forget sometimes just how strange this all sounds to nonpsychics." He turned back to Melanie. "The material objects also give off energy. During periods of very strong emotion, the person's energy mixes with the energy of the object, and it leaves what psychics call a 'memory trace.' It's this that a psychic uses to get information that helps to solve a person's problem—whatever that problem may be."

"But we already know who kidnapped Melanie, Colin," Joe said. "How's this going to help?"

"It's not the crime I'm going to focus in on," Colin explained. "I'm sure that Melanie held this lamb in stressful situations involving her mother and her mother's new husband."

"Do you want me to pull the drapes and turn off the lights?" Melanie asked.

"Well, yeah, that would help cut down on some of the distractions, but leave that reading light on," Colin said. "What made you think of that?"

"I've seen a lot of psychic movies before," Melanie said with a grin.

Melanie got up and pulled the drapes. She turned off all of the lights except for a reading lamp by her bed, and rejoined them at the table.

Colin had already put the lamb to his forehead. "It's so crowded," Colin said. His voice was barely a whisper. "There's so much here to see."

"What do you mean?" Melanie asked. Her voice sounded anxious.

"There's so much energy," Colin explained. "I see so many unhappy moments."

Melanie looked at Frank and Joe. "All my life, when something bad would happen to me, I'd curl up with my lamb," she said. She turned back to Colin. "I don't think I ever hugged it when I was happy. I had never realized that until now."

"I'll be able to sort out all the different images eventually," Colin assured her. "It'll just take more time then I thought it would."

For the next hour, they sat quietly, as Colin spoke softly to the lamb, saying things that he was hearing

153

Melanie say over the years as she tried to console herself with the stuffed animal.

After almost another hour had passed, Colin said, "I'm in the kitchen in a different house and I see a woman, who must be your mother, and I see you. Even though you're only two, I recognize you. You're sitting under the table holding the lamb close, and you're listening to the man and the woman talk. You don't want to be there, but you were playing under the table when they came in and if you come out now, the man will think you were spying on him and he'll paddle you and may even lock you in the closet. Now you're listening to what they're saying, because you just heard your name mentioned. Your mother is telling the man that she wants to move to Vermont, because she likes the colder weather, but that she's not quite sure if it would be good for you, because you have a lot of colds, and the man is frowning, and saying something about how he'd like to move there, too, because it would be far away from this place, but they can't do anything because of you. Your mother asks the man if he'll ever leave her, and the man doesn't answer. Instead, he goes out of the room, and your mother follows him. You stay under the table for a few minutes, then you leave the kitchen and go hide in the closet in your room, because you think they won't be able to find you there and take you away to this cold place called Vermont."

Colin blinked.

For several minutes, nobody said anything, then Melanie said, "I think my mother loved me. I think she was just an unhappy woman and didn't know what to do."

"I think so, too, Melanie," Colin said. "I never once felt she didn't love you."

"Do you think we should look first in Vermont, then?" Joe asked. "If Melanie was gone, there was no reason for her mother not to move there."

"I think we could start with the Internet and look for a Mary Davis or Sullivan who lives in Vermont," Frank said. "She might be listed under any of those names."

After three days of searching various Web sites, they finally found a Mary Davis Sullivan in West Middlefield, Vermont, a town just a few hours from Bayport.

"We can take you up there," Frank told Colin and Melanie. "We'll leave early Saturday morning."

"Will that be enough time for what you have in mind?" Joe asked Melanie.

Melanie nodded. "I'm getting really nervous about this. Right now, I just want to see her, maybe even from a distance, to get some idea of who she is, what she does."

Callie and Iola had been complaining for several days that Frank and Joe had been ignoring them too much lately, so when Callie mentioned that she thought it would be fun if she and Iola accompanied the boys to Vermont, Frank and Joe readily agreed.

Early Saturday morning, the six of them headed to Vermont. Melanie had her stuffed lamb with her. Two hours into the trip, they stopped for breakfast.

Melanie didn't touch her meal. "What if we don't find her?" she asked. "What then?"

Colin assured her that he wouldn't stop until they did find her.

The closer they got to West Middlefield, the more nervous Melanie got. By the time they entered the city limits, she was almost a basket case.

The Hardys were glad that Callie and Iola had come along. Their constant chatter helped relieve some of the tension and, from time to time, even made Melanie laugh.

At the first service station on their side of the road, they stopped for a map.

"Her address was listed as 423 North Essex Street," Joe said, consulting a piece of paper he had in his shirt pocket. "Do you see that on the map?"

Colin found it easily, but it was far from where they were.

Just when Frank thought they were getting close to 423, they found North Essex Street blocked by several police cars with flashing lights.

"I wonder what's going on," Joe said.

Frank parked the van on the street, and the boys got out.

"I say we find out," Frank said.

They approached one of the first patrol cars, where a police officer was leaning against the driver's door, talking on a cell phone. He said something quickly into the mouthpiece, then clicked it shut.

"We're trying to get to 423," Joe said to him. "How far up the street is it?"

The officer gave Joe a funny look. "What do you need at 423?" he asked.

"We think our friend's mother lives there," Frank explained. "She hasn't seen her in a long time. We live in Bayport. We brought her up for a visit."

"What's her mother's name?" the officer asked.

"Mary Davis Sullivan," Colin said.

The police officer snorted. "Well, you sort of picked a bad time for a visit, boys," he said. "Mary Sullivan's ex-husband is holding her hostage. There won't be any visiting today."

The police officer started to turn away, but Frank stopped him. "How are you handling this?" he asked.

The police officer frowned. "Handling this? Listen, I don't have time to discuss this with you, son. You need to move along."

"I'm Joe Hardy, and this is my brother, Frank," Joe said. "Our father is Fenton Hardy. You may have heard of him."

The Hardy boys saw a noticeable change in the police officer's demeanor.

"Oh, yeah! I know Fenton Hardy. Well, I don't actually know him," the officer said. "I heard him lecture last year in New York City. That man knows what he's talking about."

The police officer proceeded to give the boys a full account of what happened. Melanie's mother had been living in Vermont for almost fifteen years, mostly in West Middlefield. Five years ago, her husband was sent to prison, based on testimony Melanie's mother had presented in court. The husband had vowed to get even with her. He had escaped two days ago while on a work detail, had come to West Middlefield, and had taken Mrs. Sullivan hostage.

"He said there was no way she'd get out of that house alive," the officer said. "We've decided to wait them out. We think it's the best tactic."

"Thanks," Colin said. He took Frank by the arm. "I guess we'd better be getting back to Bayport."

The police officer gave him a funny look but didn't say anything.

The boys headed back to the van.

Before they got there, Joe said, "You can't be serious, Colin."

"Of course I'm not serious!" Colin said. "We're going to rescue Melanie's mother."

16 Rescue

The Hardy boys and Colin told the girls that they were going to look for a way around the roadblock, and that it would be easier for them to do it on foot than in the van.

They thought that Melanie and Iola believed them, but Frank wasn't quite sure that Callie did. The boys started down a side street before she could ask them too many questions.

It looked like there weren't as many patrol cars on the next street over, but there were still some up near where they thought 423 would be.

"Now what?" Frank said.

Joe looked at Colin. "This is your gig," he said. "Do you have any kind of a plan?"

"I'm flying by the seat of my pants," Colin said. "Just running on adrenaline."

"Sometimes that's the best way," Frank said.

The boys started walking up the sidewalk toward where the patrol cars were parked. When they got to 419, Colin said, "Let's cut behind this house and see how the alley looks."

They were thankful that 419 had lots of trees and shrubs that gave them plenty of cover. They also noticed that all of the drapes and curtains in all the houses they passed were closed, so there wasn't too much chance that they would be seen.

They were also lucky that the backyard of 419 wasn't home to some massive and unfriendly dog.

Once in the alley, they had even more luck. There were no police officers in sight.

"It'll be the third house from this one," Frank whispered. "419, 421, then 423."

They started running, staying low. When they reached the back gate of 423 North Essex Street, they lay flat on the ground for several seconds, mainly waiting to see if anyone would start shooting at them. When nothing happened, Frank reached up and tried the back gate. It opened easily.

"I'll hold it open, just wide enough for you two to slip inside, then I'll follow," Frank said. "We need to stay along the side of the fence until we reach the house."

They hadn't counted on disturbing a bird's nest

in a bush just inside the yard. The squawking produced a noise loud enough to be heard inside Mrs. Sullivan's house. It also made them run faster than they had ever run before.

They got to the side of the house just in time.

The back door opened, and a man stuck his head outside. Frank could see that he was holding a rifle. Fortunately, the man didn't look in their direction. He muttered, "Stupid birds!" and stepped back into the house.

The boys were crouched under a window. Slowly, Joe raised his head until he could see inside the room. He could tell that it was the dining room. There was a woman sitting at the table, head bowed, a cup of coffee in front of her. At that moment, Mr. Sullivan entered the room and started pacing back and forth.

"He's going to crack soon," Joe said to Frank and Colin.

"I'm going in," Colin said. He started to stand up but Frank pulled him back down.

"No, you're not," Frank said. "We're in this together, but we've got to have a plan."

Joe was looking at the grass in the backyard. It obviously hadn't been mowed in a week or so. In the corner nearest them, there was an old push mower, the kind you hardly ever saw anymore, in this age of riding mowers. Suddenly, he had an idea.

"Audacity!" Joe whispered.

Colin looked at him. "What?"

"It's a word we discussed last week in English," Joe said. "It means 'a display of daring.'"

"What's that got to do with rescuing Melanie's mother?" Colin asked.

"You do something so daring, that it catches a person totally unaware," Joe explained, "and before the person can react, you've accomplished your goal!"

"This is sounding more and more interesting," Frank said. "Keep going."

Joe told them his theory about the yard. "I'm sure it hasn't been mowed since Mr. Sullivan has been here, and I doubt Mrs. Sullivan has discussed it with him," Joe explained, "so if some goofy teenagers came up to the back door, laughing and talking about how they were sorry that they hadn't gotten around to mowing the lawn, because they've been too busy with other things, and that if it's okay, they'll go ahead and do it now, because they'll be too busy next week, then . . ." Joe paused. "You get the picture."

"Yes!" Colin agreed. "By the time Mr. Sullivan reacts, it'll be too late."

"Exactly," Joe said. He turned to Frank. "Well?"

"I think it'll work," Frank said, "but we can't stop talking for even a second, or we're dead."

They took a deep breath, stood up, and on the count of three, they started laughing and talking and shouting for Mrs. Sullivan.

When they reached the back door, they started knocking on it as hard as they could and calling, "Mrs. Sullivan! Mrs. Sullivan! We're here to mow the lawn."

They could detect a lot of movement inside, but in a few minutes, a startled and very puzzled Mrs. Sullivan opened the back door and stared at them.

They went into their routine. In the middle of it, Colin pulled open the door and said, "I'll get that pitcher of cold lemonade that you always keep for us out of the refrigerator."

"Hey, Colin! Great idea!" Joe said. He was following Colin inside. "I hope you baked those chocolate chip cookies for us. We can't mow the lawn without chocolate chip cookies."

"I'm not going to let you two near that lemonade or those cookies," Frank said with a high laugh that surprised even him. "I'm going to make sure you bring them back outside."

Now all three of the boys were inside the house. In the corner of the room, they saw Mr. Sullivan. They could tell he didn't know what to do. They made sure they kept in constant motion and didn't stare at him, but they did acknowledge him with a, "Hello, sir! We're the guys who mow the lawn, but we sure flaked out this week. Sorry!"

Mrs. Sullivan stayed where she was, at the back door, staring uncomprehendingly at the incredible performance.

Out of the corner of his eye, Frank saw Mr. Sullivan start to move toward him. It was all right, because Frank was sure that he wouldn't do anything until his mind allowed him to comprehend what was going on—and that was when the boys would make their move.

Joe and Colin had gone straight to the kitchen, and were looking in the refrigerator.

Frank got to the middle of the kitchen, made eye contact with Joe and Colin, and stopped.

Mr. Sullivan was now at the kitchen door. He slowly began to raise his rifle.

"Now!" Frank shouted.

At that moment, Joe and Colin stood up and started throwing the contents of the refrigerator at Mr. Sullivan. He sank to the floor, covered with mustard, mayonnaise, ketchup, and pickles. Later, they all agreed that it was the big jar of mayonnaise that actually did him in.

With Mr. Sullivan on the floor bleeding from glass cuts, Frank grabbed the rifle, and ran to the front door. He opened it slowly. "This is Frank Hardy! My father is Fenton Hardy!" he shouted. "Mr. Sullivan is down! Mr. Sullivan is down!"

The next few minutes were a blur.

The police swarmed into Mrs. Sullivan's house and took Mr. Sullivan into custody. At first they were really angry at the boys, but the police officer they had talked to earlier let everyone know that the Hardy boys knew exactly what they were doing and that the West Middlefield Police Department should allow the boys to do their thing.

When they saw all of the commotion, Callie, Iola, and Melanie ran down the street and, seeing the police officers swarming the house and realizing that it was 423, entered the house.

"I knew it! I knew it!" Callie said when she saw Frank. She gave him a playful punch on the shoulder. "We were worried about you guys."

"We're fine," Frank said.

After the police had been assured that Mrs. Sullivan was all right and that the Hardy boys and their friends would help her clean up her house, they left. On their way out, they told her that some other officers would be by later that day to take a statement from her.

Colin took Melanie's hand and he led her and Mrs. Sullivan into a back room. They were gone for a long time—long enough, in fact, for the Hardys, with Callie and Iola's help, to clean up the mess they had made in the kitchen.

Two hours later, Colin emerged from the room with Melanie. Mrs. Sullivan wasn't with them.

"Well?" Callie said.

"I'll tell you what I think just happened later," Frank said.

As they started down the street toward the van, Melanie gave them a sly smile, but said nothing.

Joe couldn't contain himself any longer. "Okay. What happened?" he said. "What's the story?"

"We're going to write for a while, maybe talk on the telephone," Melanie said. "We're just going to take it easy. It's been really difficult on both of us."

"I can't even imagine!" Iola said.

"Wait, Melanie. You forgot your stuffed lamb!" Callie said. "You left it at Mrs. Sullivan's house."

"No, I didn't forget it. I gave it to her," Melanie said. "I don't need it anymore."

Suddenly, Joe's skin felt all tingly. He thought he could *hear* someone talking about Mr. and Mrs. Randles. He looked over at Frank. Frank nodded at him. Joe knew that Frank was experiencing *clairaudience*, too.

"I'm feeling some energy," Joe said to Colin. He looked at Melanie. "I think someone has some really good news to tell us!"

Melanie blinked. "We do, but how—"

"Mr. Johnson is going to call Callie's father and tell him to rehire Colin's parents," Frank said. "His whole family may be moving back to Bayport."

Callie and Iola gasped.

"How did you know that?" Callie said.

Frank and Joe shrugged and gave the girls big grins.

"Maybe you guys won't need me in your agency after all," Colin said to the Hardy boys. "You already have two detectives who are psychic!"

166

Test your detective skills with these spine-tingling Aladdin Mysteries!

The Star-Spangled Secret
By K. M. Kimball

Secret of the Red Flame
By K. M. Kimball

Scared Stiff
By Willo Davis Roberts

O'Dwyer & Grady
Starring in Acting Innocent
By Eileen Heyes

Ghosts in the Gallery
By Barbara Brooks Wallace

The York Trilogy By Phyllis Reynolds Naylor

Shadows on the Wall

Faces in the Water

Footprints at the Window

Exciting fiction from three-time Newbery Honor author Gary Paulsen

Newbery Honor Book

Newbery Honor Book

Aladdin Paperbacks
Simon & Schuster Children's Publishing
www.SimonSaysKids.com